GREAT ILLUSTRATED CLASSICS

LITTLE MERMAID
& Other Stories

BARONET BOOKS, New York, New York

GREAT ILLUSTRATED CLASSICS

edited by
Rochelle Larkin

Contents

A Horrible Plague

THE · PIED · PIPER

O nce upon a time, there was a wealthy town called Hamelin. The people there worked very hard and made a lot of money. But they were all too greedy.

The greediest of all was the mayor of Hamelin. "A penny saved is a penny earned" was his favorite slogan.

But one day a horrible plague visited Hamelin — a plague of rats. The rats ate everything. They ate all the food in the kitchens and shops. They gnawed through the clothes in the closets. They chewed through all the books in the library. They even scratched the paintings on the walls. Nothing in town was as it should be.

Everyone in Hamelin was frantic. All agreed: "The rats must go!"

"But how do we get rid of them?" they wondered.

Then an old man spoke up. "There is a man who can do it. He is a magician who can pipe away any plague with his magic flute. We should write to him."

Soon the letter reached the Piper. He read it slowly and carefully. Slowly and carefully a smile spread across his face. Slowly and carefully he sent a letter of his own in reply.

The next day without any delay, he left for Hamelin with his magic flute tucked under his arm. When he arrived he met with the mayor.

"You must help us," begged the mayor. "The rats are destroying us."

"I can help you," answered the Piper. "But in return for my work you must give me nine gold coins and ninety silver coins."

"That is a large price to pay," said the mayor. "Yet if you can rid us of the rats it is well worth it."

When the price had been agreed on, the Piper strolled down the main street of town, took out his magic flute and began playing.

"What beautiful music," everyone said. All the people of Hamelin rushed to their windows to watch the Piper and listen to his lovely melodies.

But the rats loved the music best of all. They stopped whatever they were doing and followed the Piper. They were caught like fish in a net. Soon too many to even count followed the Pied Piper through the streets. They followed him on the straight roads and the curved roads, on the wide roads and the narrow roads, up and down the hilly roads.

The wily Piper played and played and the rats followed and followed. Soon he led the rats out of the town and toward the

The Piper Began Playing.

river. He walked right into the river and rats still followed. All the rats drowned.

"Well, that is that," said the Piper and smiled his slow and careful smile.

Everyone cheered his return. But then the trouble started. The mayor and the other greedy people of the town did not want to pay the Piper.

"All you have done is play a little music. For that you deserve one gold coin, and even that is too much."

"Keep your money! You'll pay for your greed!" shouted the Piper.

He ran back into the streets of Hamelin, unpacking his flute as he went. The Pied Piper was playing his music once more, but now a different melody, livelier and bouncier than he played for the rats.

This time the boys and girls of the town acted just as the rats did. They stopped whatever they were doing and danced after the Piper.

"Stop, children, stop! Come back at once," called their fathers and mothers.

But the children only heard the Piper's magic flute. Soon all the children had left the town.

"What has happened to our sons and daughters?" the people cried. "What can we do to get our children back?"

"I don't know," said the mayor. But he realized that the Pied

"One Gold Coin!"

Piper had revenged himself on the people of Hamelin.

And then the Pied Piper himself appeared.

"This is your fault," he told the mayor. "See how easy now it is to get your children back."

"Has all this happened because you refused to pay him?" asked the mayor's wife.

"I was trying to save money," whispered the mayor. "A penny saved is a penny earned."

"And look what your greed has cost us," returned his wife. "You have to pay the Piper."

"You have to pay the Piper!" shouted the townsfolk.

Once he had received his agreed upon fee, the Piper set off, again playing his flute. And soon the the children of Hamelin came back safe. The mayor and the people learned never to be greedy again, thanks to the lesson the Pied Piper taught. From then on Hamelin became known as a generous place of love and charity.

The Children Came Safely Home.

The Marble Figure from the Wreck

THE · LITTLE · MERMAID

by Hans Christian Andersen

W here the sea is deepest lies the palace of the Ocean King, who had been a widower many years. His old mother managed his household affairs for him, particularly her grand-daughters, the little Ocean Princesses. They were six beautiful children; the youngest Princess, however, was the loveliest of all, but, like all mermaids, she had no feet, her body ending in a tail like a fish.

In front of the palace was a large garden where each of the little Princesses had her own flower bed which she could plant as she liked. One laid hers out in the form of a whale, another liked that of a mermaid better; but the youngest made hers quite round, like the sun, and planted in it only flowers that were red, to resemble it in color, too. She was an extraordinary child, very quiet and thoughtful. While her sisters were adorning themselves with all sorts of things as ornaments, which they had got from a ship that had been wrecked, she asked only for the beautiful marble figure of a boy which had been found in the vessel. She placed this statue in her garden, and planted a red weeping willow beside it.

Nothing delighted the little Princess so much as to hear of the world above the waters. Her old grandmother would tell all that she knew about ships and towns, men and land-animals.

"When you have reached your fifteenth year," said the old lady, "you may rise up to the surface of the sea, sit in the moonlight, and see the large ships sail by, and become acquainted with men and cities."

The following year the eldest sister would attain this happy age; but as to her sisters, unfortunately one was always a year younger than the other, and the youngest had to wait five whole years before the glad moment should come for her to rise and behold how the upper world did look.

Each promised the others to tell what she had seen, and what she thought most beautiful, for really their grandmother told them so very little, and there were so many things that they wanted to know; besides what she told them only excited their curiosity to see the wonders with their own eyes.

But none of the sisters felt so lively a longing for this day as the youngest; she who must wait longest, and who always was so quietly absorbed in thought. Many a night she stood at the open window, and look upwards through the clear blue water, while the fishes were splashing and playing around her.

She could see the sun and the moon, in dimmed brightness

Nothing Delighted the Little Princess So Much.

only; but to her they seemed larger than they do to dwellers on earth. If a shadow concealed them, she knew that it was either a whale or a passing ship with human beings upon it, who certainly little thought that, far below, a little ocean-maiden stretched her hands upwards towards the keel of their ship, with an ardent longing to be with them.

The day now arrived when the oldest Princess reached her fifteenth year, and was to rise to the surface of the sea.

At her return she had a thousand things to relate; her greatest enjoyment had been to sit on a sand-bank in the moonlight, and to see the large city on the coast, where lights like stars were shining, music sounding, and where the noise and hum of carriages and men might be heard afar. Then, too, to behold the high church towers, and to hear the chime of the bells — it was for these she felt the greatest longing, because they were beyond her reach.

How attentively did her youngest sister listen to these words! And when she next stood by night at her open window, and looked upwards through the blue flood, she thought so intensely of the great noisy city, that she fancied she could hear the sound of the church bells.

The following year the next sister rose to the surface, to swim whither she pleased. She rose to the top of the water as the sun was going down; and this sight so delighted her, that she said, of all she had seen above the sea, this was the most magnificent.

"The whole heaven was like gold," said she, "and the beauty of the clouds is out of my power to describe: now red, now violet,

A Thousand Things to Relate

on they sailed above me; a flock of white swans flew over the water at the very spot where the sun was descending."

It was now the third sister's turn to visit the upper world. She was the most beautiful and the boldest of the three, and swam up a river that fell into the sea. Here she saw green hills with grape-vines, castles and houses among the woods; she heard the birds singing; the sun shone so warm, that she had often to dive beneath the water to cool her burning face.

In a small bay she found a whole company of little children who were bathing and jumped and splashed in the water. She wished to join them, but the children fled frightened to the land, and a little black animal barked so at her, that she grew afraid, and swam back again to the sea. But she could not forget the green woods, the leafy hills, and the little children who swam about in the water although they had no fins.

The fourth sister was not so bold; she remained in the open sea; she related that there it was more beautiful than anywhere else, for one could see miles around, while the sky, like a large bell, hung over the waves. She saw ships too, but so far off that they seemed to be seagulls; while sprightly dolphins sported on the wa-ter, and whales spouted high jets into the air that looked like a thousand fountains.

The next year the fifth sister was fifteen. Her birthday was in winter, and she saw what the others had not when she went up. The sea had become green, and icebergs were swimming about its

The Third Sister's Turn

surface. These looked like pearls, she said, but were higher than the church towers on the land. She had seated herself on one of these swimming ice-pearls, and let the wind play with her long hair; but every ship had quickly hoisted its sails, and had moved quickly away.

The first time that each sister rose from the sea, she was enchanted at the many new and beautiful objects she had seen in the upper world. But now, as grown-up maidens, they had per-mission to go up as often as they liked, and it soon lost the charm of novelty. It was not long before their own home seemed much more delightful than the upper world.

Many an evening did the five sisters, arm-in-arm, rise to the surface of the sea. When they swam on the tops of the waves, the youngest remained quite alone in her father's palace, looking after them; and at such times she felt as though she could weep. But mermaids have no tears, and therefore suffer immeasurably more in their sorrow than human beings, for tears melt human sorrow.

"Oh, were I but fifteen years old!" sighed she. "I know, for certain, that I should love the upper world and the men that live upon it very dearly!"

At length her much-desired fifteenth year was here!

"Now, then, it is your turn," said the old grandmother. "Come here, that I may dress you like your sisters."

So saying, she placed a royal wreath of white lilies in her hair, whose every petal was the half of a pearl.

The Five Sisters Arm-in-Arm

She would gladly have cast aside all her finery, and taken off the heavy wreath, for the red flowers of her garden became her much better; but she dared not do so before the old lady.

"Adieu," she said, and rose out of the sea as light and as beautiful as a bubble in water.

The sun had just left the horizon as the Little Mermaid, for the first time, appeared on the surface of the ocean; but the clouds still shone golden and rose-colored, the evening star gleamed in the pale sky, the air was mild and the sea as smooth as a mirror.

A large ship with three masts lay on the tranquil waters; a single sail was hoisted, for not a breath of air was perceptible and the sailors were sitting on the yards or in the rigging. Music and song sounded from on board; and when it was dark, hundreds of lamps suddenly glittered on the ship, and it looked as if the flags of every nation were fluttering in the air.

The Little Mermaid swam to the cabin-windows, where, each time the waves lifted her, she could see through the clear glass panes. Here she saw many gaily-dressed persons; but the handsomest of all was a young Prince with large dark eyes.

He was certainly not more than sixteen. It was his birthday, which accounted for all these festivities. The seamen danced on deck; and when the young Prince appeared among them, hundreds of rockets went up in the air, turning the night into bright day, and frightening the Little Mermaid so much that she plunged beneath the water for a minute or two.

A Large Ship Lay on the Water.

But she soon peeped out again, and it now seemed as if all the stars of heaven were falling around her. Such a rain of fire she had never seen: of such arts, known but to men, she had never even dreamed. Large suns turned round, glowing fishes swam in the air, and the whole spectacle was reflected in the clear surface of the sea.

On the ship itself it was so light that one could distinguish persons distinctively — oh, how handsome the young Prince was! To many of the people he gave his hand, and joked and laughed; while the music sounded pleasantly in the silence of the night.

It was already late; however, the little Princess could not tear herself away from the sight of the ship and the handsome Prince. She remained looking through the cabin window, rocked to and fro by the waves.

But there was a roaring in the depths of the ocean, while the Princess still swam on the surface in order to see the Prince. The ship began to move more quickly, the sails were hoisted, the waves tossed, black clouds gathered over the sky, and the noise of distant thunder was heard. The sailors perceived that a storm was coming on, so they again furled the sails. Already the huge vessel rocked on the heaving sea like a mere skiff, and the waves, towering like black mountains, broke over it: but the good ship glided downwards in the hollow of the sea like a swan, and appeared again immediately riding on the crest of the waves now lashed into foam.

To the Little Mermaid this appeared very amusing: but not so to the sailors on board. The vessel creaked and groaned, and her

How Handsome the Young Prince Was!

thick ribs bent under the heavy blows of the waves against her side, while the water rushed in. For a moment the ship reeled; the main mast snapped as though it had been a reed; she capsized and filled.

Now the Little Mermaid comprehended that the people on board were in danger; for she herself was obliged to watch out for the spars and timbers that had been torn away from the ship and were now tossing about in all directions on the waves.

At this moment it became so dark that she could not distinguish anything; though when the dreadful lightning played, it was so light that she recognized everybody on the wreck. Her eyes sought the young Prince just at the moment when the ship went to pieces and sank.

At first she was glad, thinking the Prince would now come to her; but she immediately recollected that men cannot live in the water, and that the Prince could only reach her palace as a corpse. Die? No, that he should not!

She swam through the wreck that the waves were driving about in all directions, forgetful of her own danger, dived and rose again, till at last she reached the spot where the Prince, almost exhausted, kept himself with difficulty just above the water.

His eyes were already closing, and he would inevitably have been drowned if the Little Mermaid had not come to his rescue. But she seized hold of him, and, while she was driven along by the waves, bore him above the water.

Towards morning the storm abated: but no trace of the ship

The Ship Reeled, the Main Mast Snapped.

was to be seen. The sun rose as red as fire. Its first rays seemed to color the Prince's cheeks, but his eyes were still shut. The Little Mermaid kissed his forehead, and put back his wet hair from his face. He resembled the marble figure in her garden: she kissed him once more, and wished most fervently that he might revive, and that his eyes might open and look upon her.

Now she beheld the land with its high mountains, on which white snow was shining. A green wood stretched along the coast, and in front of it lay a chapel. The sea formed here a small bay, and the fine sand that had been washed up formed firm ground. Here the Mermaid swam with the seemingly dead Prince, and took care to turn his face towards the sun, that its warmth might call back his life.

In the large white building that stood before her, the bells began to sound, and many young maidens came out to walk in the garden. The little Princess hid herself behind some rock, covered her head and hair with the froth of the sea that her face might not be seen, and watched carefully to see who would approach the Prince.

It was not long before one of the young girls went towards him. She seemed quite terrified at the sight of the lifeless Prince; but, soon recovering herself, she ran back to call her sisters. The Prince revived, and smiled kindly and joyfully on all who surrounded him; but on the Little Mermaid he cast no look, for he did not know that it was to her he owed his life.

The Little Mermaid Kissed His Forehead.

And when he was taken from where she had brought him, and carried into the large building, she grew so sad that she immediately plunged beneath the water and returned sorrowfully to her father's palace.

If she had been formerly thoughtful and quiet, she was now more so. Her sisters asked her what she had seen in the world above, but she gave no answer.

She often rose of an evening near the shore where she had left the Prince; she saw how the fruits of the garden were gathered; she saw how the snow on the mountains vanished; but the Prince she never could see; and she always returned to her submarine dwelling melancholy and sad.

Her only consolation was to sit in her garden, and to embrace the little statue that resembled the handsome Prince; she tended her flowers no longer; they grew wild, covered the paths, and so twined their long stalks and leaves round the branches of the trees that the whole garden was turned into a gloomy bower.

At last no longer able to conceal her sorrow, she told her secret to one of her sisters. The other sisters now learned the secret and one recollected the Prince; she, too, had been a witness of festivities on board; she knew in what country he was to be found, and the name of his sovereign.

"Come, little sister!" said the other Princesses, and, twining their arms together, they rose in a line out of the sea just in front of the castle of the Prince.

He Was Carried Into the Large Building

THE LITTLE MERMAID

Now the little Princess knew where her dear Prince lived; and she showed herself nearly every evening, and many a night on the water. She approached nearer the land than her sisters had; she even swam the length of the narrow canal that led below the marble balcony. Here she tarried to gaze at the young Prince, who imagined himself alone in the clear moonlight.

She often saw him, too, on the water in his splendid barge, over which the many flags were flying. She listened from among the green rushes which grew on the banks, to hear his voice; and if by chance a light breeze caught her silver veil, and the fluttering was observed by those in the Prince's boat, they thought it a swan stretching out its long white wings over the water.

Many a night when the fishermen were out by torchlight, she heard them relating much good of the Prince, and the noble actions he had performed. She rejoiced greatly at having saved his life, and she remembered how his head rested on her shoulder, and how she had kissed him when he knew nothing of it, nor even dreamed of such a thing.

Dearer and dearer did the human race become to her, and more and more did she wish to belong to them. Their world seemed to her much larger than that of the sea; they could fly away in their ships over the ocean, climb to the summits of the highest mountains that reached the clouds of heaven; and their countries, bordered by woods and decked with pleasant fields, extended themselves much father than the eye of a mermaid could reach.

Now She Knew Where Her Dear Prince Lived.

There were so many things about which she would have gladly asked, but her sisters could give her no answers. So she had to have recourse to the old Queen-Mother, who was well acquainted with the upper world, which she used to call "the country above the sea."

"Does the human race live forever if the people are not drowned?" she asked her grandmother. "Do they never die, as we do who live at the bottom of the sea?"

"Yes," replied the old lady, "they must die as well as we; and besides, their lifetime is much shorter than ours. We can live to be three hundred years of age; when we die we become foam on the sea, and have not a grave here below among those we love. We have no immortal soul, we do not live again, but are like reeds that, once cut, can never more grow green. But men have a soul that lives on and which soars upward to the shining stars in heaven. As we rise out of the water to see the countries of men, so do they rise to unknown abodes in the skies, which our eyes are not permitted to behold."

"Why do we not have immortal souls?" asked the Little Mermaid. "I would give all my three hundred years to be a human creature only for a day, and then to be allowed to dwell forever in the heavenly world."

"You must not think of such a thing," answered her old grandmother. "Why, we are much better off than men, and are far happier."

"Why Do We Not Have Immortal Souls?"

"And is there nothing I can do, grandmother, to obtain an immortal soul?"

"No," answered she. "Only when a mortal loves you so much that you are more to him than father and mother; when every thought and all his love is concentrated in you, and he gives his hand to the priest to be laid in yours with the promise of everlasting constancy — only then can you become immortal; for then would his soul dissolve in yours, and you would be made a partaker of human happiness."

"But that can never happen! What in our eyes is the handsomest part of our bodies, the tail, is considered frightful by men because they know no better. According to them, one must have two awkward props to one's body, 'legs,' as they call them, in order to look well!"

Then the Little Mermaid sighed, and looked sorrowfully at the scaly part of her body.

"Let us be happy!" continued the old lady, "Tonight there is a ball at court."

But all the Little Mermaid's thoughts were occupied with the world above her: she could not forget the handsome Prince, and her grief at not possessing an immortal soul was very great. She stole away from her father's house; and while all within was merriment and joy, she sat absorbed in thought in her little neglected garden.

She heard the sound of horns, echoing from above through

The Little Mermaid Sighed.

the water, far away in the distance; and she thought, "He is about to depart for the chase — he whom I love more than anything, who occupies my thoughts incessantly, and in whose hand I would gladly lay my life! All, all, will I hazard to win him and an immortal soul! I will go to the Witch of the Sea, whom I always dreaded, but who is perhaps the only one who can counsel and assist me."

The Little Mermaid went to the roaring Maelstrom, beyond which the sorceress dwelt. She had never been that way before: no flower grew along the path, nothing but the bare sandy ground extended itself to the Maelstrom, in which the water whirled and hurled all that it seized on down into the abyss. She would have to pass through the middle of this crushing whirlpool to arrive at the territory of the Witch, and a long part of the way led through boiling ooze.

Behind this lay her house, in wood of a peculiar sort, and a strange abode it was. All the trees and bushes consisted of serpents shooting up out of the earth. The branches were long shiny arms that unceasingly stretched out in every direction. What they caught in this manner they held so tight that it could never get loose again.

The Little Mermaid stood quite horrified before this frightful wood; she had nearly turned back, her mission unaccomplished, when her thoughts fell on the Prince and the immortal soul, and inspired her with new strength.

"I Will Go to the Witch of the Sea."

She bound up her long flying hair, that the trees might not seize it and drag her towards them, and more swiftly than a fish darts through the water, she flew safely through the fearful wood. She reached a place where large sea-snails were about; and in the middle of this place stood a house built of the bones of those who had been lost at sea. Here sat the Witch, caressing a toad in the same manner as we often see persons feeding a canary. The snails she called her chickens, and allowed them to sit upon her spongy shoulders and about her neck.

"I know well what you would ask of me," said she to the little Princess; "your intention is foolish, but your wish shall be fulfilled, my pretty maiden, though it is sure to bring misfortune on you. You would get rid of your tail, and to have in its place two stilts such as men use, that the young Prince may fall in love with you, and you may get an immortal soul.

"I will prepare you a potion, with which you must swim to the land; you must then sit on the shore, and drink it. Your fish's tail will immediately fall off, and shrivel up into what men call 'legs;' but this transformation is very painful, and you will feel as if a sharp instrument were thrust through your whole body. All who behold you will say you are the most beautiful mortal they have ever seen; you will retain your gliding gait, and no dancer, be she ever so light, will move with so elastic a step; but at every motion you will suffer intolerable pain; you will feel as though you were treading on sharp blades. If you will subject yourself to all these

She Flew Through the Fearful Wood.

torments, I will grant your request."

"Yes, I will!" answered the little Princess, with trembling voice; for she thought of her beloved Prince, and of getting an immortal soul.

"But remember," said the Witch, "you can never be a mermaid again, when you have taken human form; you will never be able to descend to your sisters and your home, and should you not gain the Prince's love in such degree that, for your sake, he forgetteth father and mother, that all his thoughts and all his joy be in you, and join your hands together as man and wife — without this you will never obtain the immortality you seek. The morning after he is united to another will be the day of your death; your heart will break for grief, and you will changed into the foam on the waves of the sea."

"I still will venture!" continued the Little Mermaid, pale and trembling like on the point of death.

"But I must be paid, too, and it is no trifle that I require of you for my trouble. You have the most charming voice of all the dwellers in the sea, and with it you reckon to captivate the Prince; but this voice I must have. The best of your possessions I demand for my miraculous potion; for I must give of my own blood to impart to the mixture the sharpness of a two-edged sword."

"But if you take my voice from me," said the Princess, "what have I left to captivate the Prince?"

"Your lovely form," answered the Witch; "your light airy

"You Can Never Be a Mermaid Again."

step, and your expressive eyes. These are surely enough to befool a poor human heart! Well, what do you say? Have you lost your courage? Come, that I may take it for myself in exchange for my magic drink."

"Be it so!" answered the Princess.

The Witch set her cauldron on the fire to seeth the charmed potion. "Cleanliness is a principal thing," said she, and let the blood drop into the vessel. Every moment the Witch threw in new ingredients; and when the cauldron boiled, sighs rose resembling the wail of the crocodile. At last the mixture was ready, and was transparent as pure water as she poured it into a vial.

"There it is," said the Witch to the Princess; and at the same moment she took her voice. The Little Mermaid was thus made dumb; she could neither speak nor sing.

She now looked once again at her father's palace; the lamps in the ballroom were extinguished, and all her family were doubtless gone to rest. She would not enter, as she was unable to speak, and was, besides, on the point of leaving her home forever. At the thought her heart was well-nigh broken; she glided into the garden, picked a flower from the bed of each sister as a remembrance, waved with her hand many a farewell towards the palace, and then rose through the dark blue waters to the upper world.

She reached the Prince's dwelling, and ascended the well-known marble steps. And now the Little Mermaid emptied the vial with the piercing potion, which convulsed her whole frame:

"Be It So!"

she felt it pass through her like the thrust of a sword, and it affected her so that she sank lifeless on the ground.

When the sun rose she awoke, and felt a burning pain in every limb; but before her stood the object of her fervent love, the handsome young Prince, with his dark eyes upon her. She looked down and saw that, in place of her long fish-like tail the finest legs were grown.

The Prince asked who she was, and from where she came; and, smiling sweetly, she looked at him with her bright blue eyes, for she could speak no more. He then took her hand, and led her into his castle. At every step it was as the Witch had said — as though she was treading on sharpcutting blades; but she bore the pain willingly. She moved along beside the Prince like a zephyr; and all who saw her wondered at the charming grace and lightness of her every movement.

When she had entered the palace, robes of costly silk were handed to her, and she was the most lovely among the ladies of the court, though she could speak and sing no longer. Female musicians dressed in silk and gold brocade now came to sing before the Prince and his royal parents. One was particularly distinguished by her beautiful clear voice; and the Prince showed his approval by clapping his hands. This made the Little Mermaid quite sad, for she knew she could have sung much better if her voice had not been taken from her.

"Oh," thought she in silence, "if he did but know that for his

The Finest Legs Were Grown.

sake I have sacrificed my voice forever!"

They now began to dance. The dainty Little Mermaid stretched out her delicate arms, and danced with such an air as had never been seen before. With every movement the lovely grace of her body seemed more apparent, and the expression which beamed in her eyes appealed to the heart of the spectators far more movingly than the songs of the female musicians.

All present were enchanted with her, but especially the young Prince, who called her his dear little foundling. And she danced again, and more beautifully still, although at every step she was obliged to bear the cutting knives; and the Prince said she should always remain in his palace; and an apartment was prepared for her, provided with graceful furniture, and a bed of velvet cushions.

And the Prince had a riding-dress made for her, that she might accompany him on horseback; and they rode together through the fragrant woods, where the green boughs touched their shoulders, and the little birds rejoiced from behind the fresh leaves. With the Prince, too, she climbed the highest mountains; and although her delicate feet bled as she went on, so that the attendants saw it, she only smiled, and still followed her dear Prince up on high, where she saw the clouds chasing each other beneath them like a flock of birds passing to other lands.

At night, when all the palace was asleep, she would descend the marble steps to cool her feet in the refreshing sea; and she thought then of her dear ones in the deep.

The Little Mermaid Stretched Out Her Arms

Once, while she was standing there, her sisters came swimming by, arm-in-arm, and their singing was most melancholy. She beckoned to them, and her sisters recognized her, and told her how great had been the mourning for her in their father's house.

Henceforward they visited their sister every night, and once brought with them their old grandmother, who for many years had not been in the upper world, and their father too, the Ocean King, with the crown upon his head. But the two did not venture so near the land as to be able to speak to her.

Each day the Little Mermaid grew dearer to the Prince; he loved her like a good dear child; but to make her his wife never even entered his thoughts; and yet she must become his wife before she could obtain an immortal soul; and his wife she must be, or be changed into foam and be driven restlessly and forever over the billows of the sea.

"But do you not care most for me?" her eyes seemed to say.

"Yes," said the Prince, "you are dearer to me than all beside; for in goodness there is none like you. You are devoted and you resemble a maid that I once saw standing before me, but shall probably never behold again. I was on board a ship that was wrecked in a sudden storm; the waves threw me on the shore near a sacred temple, in which were many maidens. The youngest of them saved my life. I saw her but once; yet her image is vivid before my eyes — she is the only one I can ever love. But you are so like her — you almost drive her remembrance from me! But she

They Did Not Venture So Near the Land

belongs to the holy temple, and my good fortune has given me you as a consolation. Never, never will we be parted!"

"Oh, he does not know that it was I who saved his life!" thought the Little Mermaid with a sigh. "I bore him over the wild flood to the grove where the temple stands; I sat behind the rocks, and saw the beauteous maiden whom he loves more than me." And she sighed deeply at these words; for she could not weep. "She belongs to the holy temple, he says; she never goes into the world; she will never meet him again. But I am near him; I see him daily; I love him, and to him will I devote my whole life."

"The Prince will soon wed the daughter of our neighbor King," said the people: "and that's the reason why the stately ship is being got ready. 'Tis true, they say he is going to travel through the country; but the real reason is to see the Princess. That is the cause of his taking such a large retinue with him." But the Little Mermaid laughed at these conjectures; for she knew the Prince's intentions better than any one.

"I must make a journey," said he to her; "I must go and see the beautiful Princess. My parents require me to do so; but force me to marry her — to bring her back as my betrothed — that they will never do. Besides, it is impossible for me to love the Princess; for she cannot be as like the lovely maiden of the temple as you are; and if I am to choose, I would rather take thee, my little silent foundling, with the speaking eyes!" And he kissed her, and then she dreamed a sweet vision of mortal happiness and of an immortal soul.

"But You Are So Like Her!"

"You do not fear the water, my child?" asked he tenderly, as she stood on the splendid ship that was to convey him to the territories of the neighboring monarch.

And then he told her of storms at sea, and of calms, or rare fish that inhabited the deep, and what divers had seen below. But she smiled as his words: for she knew better than any mortal creature how it looked, and what went on, in the depths of the ocean.

In the moonlit night, when all on board slept except the man at the helm, she sat at the bow and looked over the ship's side into the sea. It seemed to her as though she could see her father's palace and her old grandmother with her silver crown, as she gazed down into the waters.

And then her sisters appeared upon the waves, looked at her with sorrowful expression, and stretched out their arms towards her. She beckoned to them, smiled, and would have told them by signs that she was happy; but just at that moment the cabin-boy approached, and the sisters dived down so suddenly that the boy thought the white appearance he saw upon the surface of the water was the foam of the sea.

The next morning the ship entered the harbor of the splendid capital of the neighboring King. The bells rang a merry peal, and the clarions sounded from the high towers, while the soldiers in the streets paraded with waving colors and glittering arms.

Each day brought with it some new festival. But the Princess had not yet arrived in the town: she had been educated in a con-

She Stood on the Splendid Ship.

vent far off, where she had been taught the exercise of all royal virtues. At last she came.

The Little Mermaid was curious to see her beauty; and she was forced to acknowledge that she had never on earth beheld more noble features. The skin of the Princess was so fair and delicate and from behind her dark lashes smiled a pair of deep-brown eyes.

"It is herself!" exclaimed the Prince, on beholding her. "Thou art she who saved my life when I lay senseless on the shore!

"Oh, now I am more than happy!" said he to his little foundling. "That which I never hoped to see fulfilled has happened. Thou wilt rejoice at my happiness; for thou lovest me more than all who surround me."

Then the Little Mermaid kissed his hand in her sorrow, and she thought her heart would break; for the dawn of his marriage-day was to bring her unavoidable death.

And again the church bells rang, and heralds rode through the streets and announced the approaching wedding of the Princess. Flames burnt out of silver vases on every altar; bride and bridegroom gave each other their hands while the clergyman blessed the holy union.

The Little Mermaid, clad in silk and cloth of gold, stood behind the Princess and held the train of her bridal dress; but her ear heard not the solemn music, and her eye saw nothing of it. She flung herself into the sea, and she felt her body gradually dissolving into foam.

"It Is Herself!"

And the Little Mermaid stretched her transparent arms upwards to the sun, and, for the first time in her life, tears wetted her eyes.

And on the ship all were rejoicing; she saw the Prince and his lovely bride, and watched how both sought after her. Sorrowfully they looked at the froth of the sea, as if they knew that she had plunged into the waves. Unseen she kissed the bridegroom's forehead, smiled at him, and then rose with the air, and soared high above the rosy clouds that floated so peacefully.

The Little Mermaid Stretched Her Arms Upward to the Sun.

"If Only We Had!"

PRINCE · RABBIT

O nce upon a time there was a King who had no children. Sometimes he would say to the Queen, "If only we had a son!" And the Queen would answer, "If only we had!" And then on another day he would say, "If only we had a daughter!" And the Queen would sigh and answer, "Yes, if we had a daughter, that would be something." But they had no children at all.

As the years went on, and there were still no children in the Royal Palace, the people began to ask each other who would be the next King to reign over them. And some said that perhaps it would be the Chancellor, which was a pity, as nobody liked him very much; and others said that there would be no King at all, but that everybody would be equal. Those who were lowest of all thought that this would be a satisfactory ending of the matter; but those who were higher up felt that, though in some respects it would be a good thing, yet in other respects it would be an ill-advised state of affairs; and they hoped, therefore, that a young Prince would be born in the Palace. But no Prince was born.

One day, when the Chancellor was in audience with the King, it seemed well to him to speak what was in the people's minds.

"Your Majesty," he said and then stopped, wondering how best to put it.

"Well?" said the King.

"Have I your Majesty's permission to speak my mind?"

"So far yes," said the King.

Encouraged by this, the Chancellor resolved to put the matter plainly.

"In the event of your Majesty's death — " He coughed and began again. "If your Majesty ever *should* die," he said, "which in any case will not be for many years — if ever — as, I need hardly say, your Majesty's loyal subjects earnestly hope — I mean they hope it will be never. But assuming for the moment — making the sad assumption — "

"You said you wanted to speak your mind," interrupted the King. "Is this it?"

"Yes, your Majesty."

"Then I don't think much of it."

"Thank you, your Majesty."

"What you are trying to say is, 'Who will be the next King?' "

"Quite so, your Majesty."

"Ah!" The King was silent for a little. Then he said, "I can tell you who won't be."

The Chancellor did not seek for information on this point,

"Then I Don't Think Much of It."

feeling that in the circumstances the answer was obvious.

"What do you suggest yourself?"

"That your Majesty choose a successor from among the young and highly born of the country, putting him to whatever test seems good to your Majesty."

The King pulled at his beard and frowned.

"There must be not one test, but many tests. Let all who will offer themselves, provided only that they are under the age of twenty and are well-born. See to it."

He waved his hand in dismissal, and with an accuracy established by long practice the Chancellor retired backwards out of the Palace.

On the following morning, therefore, it was announced that all those who were ambitious to be appointed the King's successor, and who were of high birth and not yet come to the age of twenty, should present themselves a week later for the tests to which His Majesty desired to put them, the first of which was to be a running race. Whereat the people rejoiced, for they wished to be ruled by one to whom they could look up, and running was much esteemed in that country.

On the appointed day the excitement was great. All along the course, which was once round the castle, large crowds were massed, and at the finishing point the King and Queen themselves were seated in a specially erected pavilion. And to this pavilion the competitors were brought to be introduced to their Majesties. And

The Chancellor Retired Backwards Out of the Palace.

there were nine young nobles, well-built, and handsome, and (it was thought) intelligent, who were competitors. And there was also one Rabbit.

The Chancellor had first noticed the Rabbit when he was lining up the competitors, pinning numbers on their backs so that the people could identify them, and giving them such instructions as seemed necessary to him. "Now, now, be off with you," he had said. "Competitors only, this way." And he had made a motion of impatient dismissal with his foot.

"I *am* a competitor," said the Rabbit. "And I don't think it is usual," he added with dignity, "for the starter to kick one of the competitors just at the beginning of an important foot-race. It looks like favoritism."

"You can't be a competitor," laughed all the young nobles.

"Why not? Read the rules."

The Chancellor, feeling rather hot suddenly, read the rules. The Rabbit was certainly under twenty; he had a pedigree which showed that he was of the highest birth; and —

"And," said the Rabbit, "I am ambitious to be appointed the King's successor. Those were all the conditions. Now let's get on with the race."

But first came the introduction to the King. One by one the competitors came up . . . and at the end —

"This," said the Chancellor, as airily as he could, "is Rabbit."

Rabbit bowed in the most graceful manner possible; first to

There was also One Rabbit.

the King and then to the Queen. But the King only stared at him. Then he turned to the Chancellor.

"Well?"

The Chancellor shrugged his shoulders.

"His entry does not appear to lack validity," he said.

"He means, your Majesty, that it is all right," explained Rabbit.

The King laughed suddenly. "Go on," he said. "We can always have a race for a new Chancellor afterwards."

So the race was started. And the young Lord Calomel was much cheered on coming in second; not only by their Majesties, but also by Rabbit, who had finished the course some time before, and was now lounging in the Royal Pavilion.

"A very good style, your Majesty," said Rabbit, turning to the King. "Altogether he seems to be a most promising youth."

"Most," said the King grimly. "So much so that I do not propose to trouble the rest of the competitors. The next test shall take place between you and him."

"Not racing again, please, your Majesty. That would hardly be fair to his lordship."

"No, not racing; fighting."

"Ah! What sort of fighting?"

"With swords," said the King.

"I am a little rusty with swords, but I daresay in a day or two — "

"It will be now," said the King.

Lord Calomel Comes in Second.

"You mean, your Majesty, as soon as Lord Calomel has re-covered his breath?"

The King answered nothing, but turned to his Chancellor.

"Tell the young Lord Calomel that in half an hour I desire him to fight with this Rabbit — "

"The young Lord Rabbit," murmured the other competitor to the Chancellor.

"To fight with him for my kingdom."

"*And* borrow me a sword, will you?" said Rabbit. "Quite a small one. I don't want to hurt him."

So, half an hour later, on a level patch of grass in front of the pavilion, the fight began. It was a short, but exciting, struggle. Calomel, whirling his long sword in his strong right arm, dashed upon Rabbit, and Rabbit, carrying his short sword in his teeth, dodged between Calomel's legs and brought him toppling.

And when it was seen that the young Lord rose from the ground with a broken arm, and that with the utmost gallantry he had now taken his sword in his left hand, the people cheered. And Rabbit, dropping his sword for a moment, cheered, too; and then he picked it up and got it entangled in his adversary's legs again, so that again the young Lord Calomel crashed to the ground, this time with a sprained ankle. And there he lay.

Rabbit trotted into the Royal Pavilion, and dropped his sword in the Chancellor's lap.

"Thank you so much," he said. "Have I won?"

A Short, But Exciting, Struggle

The King frowned and pulled at his beard.

"There are other tests," he muttered.

But what were they to be? It was plain that Lord Calomel was in no condition for another physical test. What, then, of an intellectual test?

"After all," said the King to the Queen that night, "intelligence is a quality not without value to a ruler."

"Is it?" asked the Queen doubtfully.

"I have found it so," said the King, a little haughtily.

"Oh," said the Queen.

"There is a riddle, of which my father was fond, the answer to which has never been revealed save to the Royal House. We might make this the final test between them."

"What is the riddle?"

"I fancy it goes like this." He thought for a moment, and then recited it, beating time with his hand.

> "My *first* I do for your delight,
>
> Although 'tis neither black nor white.
>
> My *second* looks the other way,
>
> Yet always goes to bed by day.
>
> My *whole* can fly, and climb a tree,
>
> And sometimes swims upon the sea."

"What is the answer?" asked the Queen.

"As far as I remember," said His Majesty, "it is either *Dormouse* or *Raspberry*."

"The Answer Has Never Been Revealed."

" 'Dormouse' doesn't make sense," objected the Queen.

"Neither does 'raspberry,' " pointed out the King.

"Then how can they guess it?"

"They can't. But my idea is that young Calomel should be secretly told beforehand what the answer is, so that he may win the competition."

"Is that fair?" asked the Queen doubtfully.

"Yes," said the King. "Certainly. Or I wouldn't have suggested it."

So it was duly announced by the Chancellor that the final test between the young Lord Calomel and Rabbit would be the solving of an ancient riddle-me-ree, which in the past had baffled all save those of Royal blood. Copies of the riddle had been sent to the competitors, and in a week from that day they would be called upon to give their answers before their Majesties and the full Court. And with Lord Calomel's copy went a message, which said this:

"*From a Friend*. The answer is *Dormouse*. BURN THIS."

The day came round; and Calomel and Rabbit were brought before their Majesties; and they bowed to their Majesties, and were ordered to be seated, for Calomel's ankle was still painful to him. And when the Chancellor had called for silence, the King addressed those present, explaining the conditions of the test to them.

"And the answer to the riddle," he said, "is in this sealed paper, which I now hand to my Chancellor, in order that he shall

Announcing the Final Test

PRINCE RABBIT

open it, as soon as the competitors have told us what they know of the matter."

The people, being uncertain what else to do, cheered slightly.

"I will ask Lord Calomel first," His Majesty went on. He looked at his lordship, and his lordship nodded slightly. And Rabbit, noticing that nod, smiled suddenly to himself.

"Lord Calomel," said the King, "what do you consider to be the best answer to this riddle-me-ree?"

The young Lord Calomel tried to look very wise, and he said:

"There are many possible answers to this riddle-me-ree, but the best answer seems to be *Dormouse*."

"Let someone take a note of that answer," said the King; whereupon the Chief Secretary wrote down: "LORD CALOMEL — *Dormouse*."

"Now," said the King to Rabbit, "what suggestion have you to make in this matter?"

Rabbit, who had spent an anxious week inventing answers each more impossible than the last, looked down modestly.

"Well?" said the King.

"Your Majesty," said Rabbit with some apparent hesitation, "I have a great respect for the intelligence of the young Lord Calomel, but I think that in this matter he is mistaken. The answer is not, as he suggests, *wood-louse*, but *dormouse*."

"I *said* 'dormouse,'" cried Calomel indignantly.

"I thought you said 'wood-louse,'" said Rabbit in surprise.

Rabbit Noticing the Nod.

"He certainly said 'dormouse,' " said the King coldly.

" 'Wood-louse,' I *think*," said Rabbit.

"Lord Calomel — '*Dormouse*,' " read out the Chief Secretary.

"There you are," said Calomel. "I did say 'dormouse.' "

"My apologies," said Rabbit, with a bow. "Then we are both right, for *dormouse* it certainly is."

The Chancellor broke open the sealed paper, and to the amazement of nearly all present read out "*Dormouse*."

"Apparently, your Majesty," he said in some surprise, "they are both equally correct."

The King scowled. In some way, which he didn't quite understand, he had been tricked.

"May I suggest, your Majesty," the Chancellor went on, "that they be asked now some question of a different order, such as can be answered, after not more than a few minutes' thought, here in your Majesty's presence. Some problem in the higher mathematics, for instance, such as might be profitable for a future King to know."

"What question?" asked His Majesty, a little nervously.

"Well, as an example — what is seven times six?" And, behind his hand, he whispered to the King, "Forty-two."

Not a muscle of the King's face moved, but he looked thoughtfully at the Lord Calomel. Supposing his lordship did not know!

"Well?" he said reluctantly. "What is the answer?"

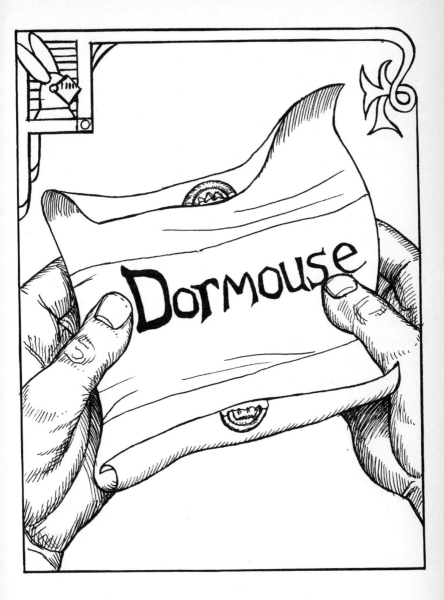

"Both Equally Correct"

The young Lord Calomel thought for some time, and then said, "Fifty-four."

"And you?" said the King to Rabbit.

Rabbit wondered what to say. As long as he gave the same answers as Calomel, he could not lose in the encounter, yet in this case "Forty-two" was the right answer. But the King, who could do no wrong, even in arithmetic, might decide, for the purposes of the competition, that "Fifty-four" was an answer more becoming to the future ruler of the country. Was it, then, safe to say "Forty-two?"

"Your Majesty," he said, "there are several possible answers to this extraordinarily novel conundrum. At first sight the obvious solution would appear to be 'Forty-two.' The objection to this solution is that it lacks originality. I have long felt that a progressive country such as ours might well strike out a new line in the matter. Let us agree that in future seven sixes are fifty-four. In that case the answer, as Lord Calomel has pointed out, *is* 'Fifty-four.' But if your Majesty would prefer to cling to the old style of counting, then your Majesty and your Majesty's Chancellor would make the answer 'Forty-two.'"

After saying which, Rabbit bowed gracefully, both to their Majesties and to his opponent, and sat down again.

The King scratched his head in a puzzled sort of way.

"The correct answer," he said, "is, or will be in the future, 'Fifty-four.'"

Fifty-four or Forty-two?

"Make a note of that," whispered the Chancellor to the Chief Secretary.

"Lord Calomel guessed this at his first attempt; Rabbit at his second attempt. I therefore declare Lord Calomel the winner."

"Shame!" said Rabbit.

"Who said that?" cried the King furiously.

Rabbit looked over his shoulder, with the object of identifying the culprit, but was apparently unsuccessful.

"However," went on the King, "in order that there should be no doubt in the minds of my people as to the absolute fairness with which this competition is being conducted, there will be one further test. It happens that a King is often called upon to make speeches and exhortations to his people, and for this purpose the ability to stand evenly upon two legs for a considerable length of time is of much value to him. The next test, therefore, will be — "

But at this point Lord Calomel cleared his throat so loudly that the King had to stop and listen to him.

"Quite so," said the King. "The next test, therefore, will be held in a month's time, when his lordship's ankle is healed, and it will be a test to see who can balance himself longest upon two legs only."

Rabbit lolloped back to his home in the wood, pondering deeply.

Now there was an enchanter who lived in the wood, a man of many magical gifts. He could (it was averred by the country-

"I Declare Lord Calomel the Winner."

side) extract colored ribbons from his mouth, cook plum-puddings in a hat, and produce as many as ten silk handkerchiefs, knotted together, from a twist of paper. And that night, after a simple dinner of salad, Rabbit called upon him.

"Can you," he said, "turn a rabbit into a man?"

The enchanter considered this carefully.

"I can," he said at last, "turn a plum-pudding into a rabbit."

"That," said Rabbit, "to be quite frank, would not be a helpful operation."

"I can turn almost anything into a rabbit," said the enchanter with growing enthusiasm. "In fact, I like doing it."

Then Rabbit had an idea.

"Can you turn a man into a rabbit?"

"I did once. At least I turned a baby into a baby rabbit."

"When was that?"

"Eighteen years ago. At the court of King Nicodemus. I was giving an exhibition of my powers to him and his good Queen. I asked one of the company to lend me a baby, never thinking for a moment that — the young Prince was handed up. I put a red silk handkerchicf over him, and waved my hands. Then I took the handkerchief away. . . . The Queen was very much distressed. I tried everything I could, but it was useless. The King was most generous about it. He said that I could keep the rabbit. I carried it about with me for some weeks, but one day it escaped. Dear, dear!" He wiped his eyes gently with a red silk handkerchief.

"I Can Turn a Plum Pudding into a Rabbit."

"Most interesting," said Rabbit. "Well, this is what I want you to do." And they discussed the matter from the beginning.

A month later the great Standing Competition was to take place. When all was ready, the King rose to make his opening remarks.

"We are now," he began, "to make one of the most interesting tests between our two candidates for the throne. At the word 'Go!' they will — " And then he stopped suddenly. "Why, what's this?" he said, putting on his spectacles. "Where is the young Lord Calomel? And what is that second rabbit doing? There was no need to bring your brother," he added severely to Rabbit.

"I am Lord Calomel," said the second rabbit meekly.

"Oh!" said the King.

"Go!" said the Chancellor, who was a little deaf.

Rabbit, who had been practising for a month, jumped on his back paws and remained there. Lord Calomel, who had no practice at all, remained on all fours. In the crowd at the back the enchanter chuckled to himself.

"How long do I stay like this?" asked Rabbit.

"This is all very awkward and distressing," said the King.

"May I get down?" said Rabbit.

"There is no doubt that the Rabbit has won," said the Chancellor.

"Which rabbit?" cried the King crossly. "They're both rabbits."

"I am Lord Calomel."

"The one with the white spots behind the ears," said Rabbit helpfully. "May I get down?"

There was a sudden cry from the back of the hall.

"Your Majesty!"

"Well, well, what is it?"

The enchanter pushed his way forward.

"May I look, your Majesty?" he said in a trembling voice. "White spots behind the ears? Dear, dear! Allow me!" He seized Rabbit's ears, and bent them this way and that.

"Ow!" said Rabbit.

"It is! Your Majesty, it is!"

"Is what?"

"The son of the late King Nicodemus, whose country is now joined to your own. Prince Silvio."

"Quite so," said Rabbit airily, hiding his surprise. "Didn't any of you recognize me?"

"Nicodemus only had one son," said the Chancellor, "and he died as a baby."

"Not died," said the enchanter, and forthwith explained the whole sad story.

"I see," said the King, when the story was ended. "But of course that is neither here nor there. A competition like this must be conducted with absolute impartiality." He turned to the Chancellor. "Which of them won that last test?"

"Prince Silvio," said the Chancellor.

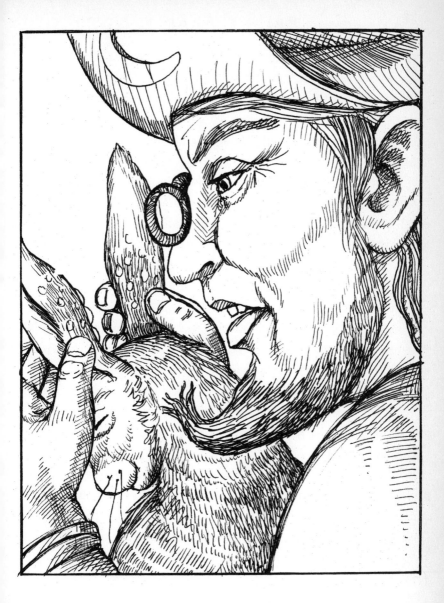

"Son of the Late King Nicodemus"

"Then, my dear Prince Silvio — "

"One moment," interrupted the enchanter excitedly. "I've just thought of the words. I *knew* there were some words you had to say."

He threw his red silk handkerchief over Rabbit, and cried, "Hey presto!"

And the handkerchief rose and rose and rose. . . .

And there was Prince Silvio!

You can imagine how loudly the people cheered. But the King appeared not to notice that anything surprising had happened.

"Then, my dear Prince Silvio," he went on, "as the winner of this most interesting series of contests, you are appointed successor to our throne."

"Your Majesty," said Silvio, "this is too much." And he turned to the enchanter and said, "May I borrow your handkerchief for a moment? My emotion has overcome me."

So on the following day, Prince Rabbit was duly proclaimed heir to the throne before all the people. But not until the ceremony was over did he return the enchanter's red handkerchief.

"And now," he said to the enchanter, "you may restore Lord Calomel to his proper shape."

And the enchanter placed his handkerchief on Lord Calomel's head, and said "Hey presto!" and Lord Calomel stretched himself and said, "Thanks very much." But he said it rather coldly, as if he were not really very grateful.

"Hey Presto!"

So they all lived happily for a long time. And Prince Rabbit married the most beautiful Princess of those parts; and when a son was born to them there was much feasting and jollification. And the King gave a great party, whereat minstrels, tumblers, jugglers and such like were present in large quantities to give pleasure to the company. But in spite of a suggestion made by the Princess, the enchanter was not present.

"But I hear he is so clever," said the Princess to her husband.

"He has many amusing inventions," replied the Prince, "but some of them are not in the best of taste."

"Very well, dear," said the Princess.

The King Gave a Great Party.

Bewailing His Sad Loss

THE · HORSE · AND · THE · SWORD

Many, many years ago there lived a King and Queen who had only one son, called Sigurd. When the little boy was only ten years old the Queen, his mother, fell ill and died, and the King, who loved her dearly, built a splendid monument to his wife's memory, and day after day he sat by it and bewailed his sad loss.

One morning, as he sat by the grave, he noticed a richly dressed lady close to him. He asked her name and she answered that it was Ingiborg; she seemed surprised to see the King there all alone. Then he told her how he had lost his Queen, and how he came daily to weep at her grave. In return, the lady informed him that she had lately lost her husband, and suggested that they might both find it a comfort if they made friends.

This pleased the King so much that he invited her to his palace, where they saw each other often, and after a time he married her.

After the wedding was over he soon regained his good spirits, and used to ride out hunting as in old days; but Sigurd, who was very fond of his stepmother, always stayed at home with her.

One evening Ingiborg said to Sigurd: "Tomorrow your father is going out hunting, and you must go with him." But Sigurd said he would much rather stay at home, and the next day when the King rode off Sigurd refused to accompany him. The stepmother was very angry, but he would not listen, and at last she assured him that he would be sorry for his disobedience, and that in future he had better do as he was told.

After the hunting party had started she hid Sigurd under her bed, and bade him be sure to lie there till she called him.

Sigurd lay very still for a long while, and was just thinking it was no good staying there any more, when he felt the floor shake under him as if there were an earthquake, and peeping out he saw a great giantess wading along ankle deep through the ground and ploughing it up as she walked.

"Good morning, Sister Ingiborg," cried she as she entered the room, "is Prince Sigurd at home?"

"No," said Ingiborg; "he rode off to the forest with his father this morning." And she laid the table for her sister and set food before her.

After they were both done eating the giantess said: "Thank you, sister, for your good dinner — the best lamb and the best drink I have ever had; but — is not Prince Sigurd at home?"

Ingiborg again said, "No"; and the giantess took leave of her and went away. When she was quite out of sight Ingiborg told

Under the Bed

Sigurd to come out of his hiding place.

The King returned home at night, but his wife told him nothing of what had happened, and the next morning she again begged the Prince to go out hunting with his father. Sigurd, however, replied as before, that he would much rather stay at home.

So once more the King rode off alone. This time Ingiborg hid Sigurd under the table, and scolded him well for not doing as she bade him. For some time he lay quite still, and then suddenly the floor began to shake, and a giantess came along wading half way to her knees through the ground.

As she entered the house she asked, as the first one had done: "Well, Sister Ingiborg, is Prince Sigurd at home?"

"No," answered Ingiborg, "he rode off hunting with his father this morning"; and going to the cupboard she laid the table for her sister.

When they had finished their meal the giantess rose and said: "Thank you for all these nice dishes, and for the best lamb and the nicest drink I have ever had; but — is Prince Sigurd *really* not at home?"

"No, certainly not!" replied Ingiborg; and with that they took leave of each other.

When she was well out of sight Sigurd crept from under the table, and his stepmother declared that it was most important that he should not stay at home the next day; but he said he did not see what harm could come of it, and he did not mean to go out hunt-

A Giantess Came Along.

ing, and the next morning, when the King prepared to start, Ingiborg implored Sigurd to accompany his father.

But it was all no use. He was quite obstinate and would not listen to a word she said. "You will have to hide me again," said he, so no sooner had the King gone than Ingiborg hid Sigurd between the wall and the panelling, and by-and-by there was heard once more a sound like an earthquake, as a great giantess, wading knee deep through the ground, came in at the door.

"Good day, Sister Ingiborg!" she cried, in a voice like thunder; "is Prince Sigurd at home?"

"Oh, no," answered Ingiborg, "he is enjoying himself out there in the forest. I expect it will be quite dark before he comes back again."

"That's a lie!" shouted the giantess. And they squabbled about it till they were tired, after which Ingiborg laid the table; and when the giantess had done eating she said: "Well, I must thank you for all these good things, and for the best lamb and the best drink I have had for a long time; but — are you *quite* sure Prince Sigurd is not at home?"

"Quite," said Ingiborg. "I've told you already that he rode off with his father this morning to hunt in the forest."

At this the giantess roared out with a terrible voice: "If he is near enough to hear my words, I lay this spell on him: Let him be half scorched and half withered, and may he have neither rest nor peace till he finds me." And with these words she stalked off.

"Is Prince Sigurd at Home?"

For a moment Ingiborg stood as if turned to stone, then she fetched Sigurd from his hiding place, and, to her horror, there he was, half scorched and half withered.

"Now you see what has happened through your own obstinacy," said she; "but we must lose no time, for your father will soon be coming home."

Going quickly into the next room she opened a chest and took out a ball of string and three gold rings, and gave them to Sigurd, saying: "If you throw this ball on the ground it will roll along till it reaches some high cliffs. There you will see a giantess looking out over the rocks. She will call down to you and say: 'Ah, this is just what I wanted! Here is Prince Sigurd. He shall go into the pot to-night'; but don't he frightened by her.

"She will draw you up with a long boat hook, and you must greet her from me, and give her the smallest ring as a present. This will please her and she will ask you to wrestle with her. When you are exhausted, she will offer you a horn to drink out of, and though she does not know it, the wine will make you so strong that you will easily be able to conquer her. After that she will let you stay there all night.

"The same thing will happen with my two other sisters. But, above all, remember this: should my little dog come to you and lay his paws on you, with tears running down his face, then hurry home, for my life will be in danger. Now, good-bye, and don't forget your stepmother."

A Ball of String and Three Gold Rings

Then Ingiborg dropped the ball on the ground, and Sigurd bade her farewell.

That same evening the ball stopped rolling at the foot of some high rocks, and on glancing up, Sigurd saw the giantess looking out at the top.

"Ah, just what I wanted!" she cried out when she saw him; "here is Prince Sigurd. He shall go into the pot tonight. Come up, my friend, and wrestle with me."

With these words she reached out a long boat hook and hauled him up the cliff. At first Sigurd was rather frightened, but he remembered what Ingiborg had said, and gave the giantess her sister's message and the ring.

The giantess was delighted, and challenged him to wrestle with her. Sigurd was fond of all games, and began to wrestle with joy; but he was no match for the giantess, and as she noticed that he was getting faint she gave him a horn to drink out of, which was very foolish on her part, as it made Sigurd so strong that he soon overthrew her.

"You may stay here tonight," said she; and he was glad of the rest.

The next morning Sigurd threw down the ball again and away it rolled for some time, till it stopped at the foot of another high rock. Then he looked up and saw another giantess, even bigger and uglier than the first one, who called out to him: "Ah, this is just what I wanted! Here is Prince Sigurd. He shall go into the

"Come Wrestle with Me."

pot to-night. Come up quickly and wrestle with me." And she lost no time in hauling him up.

The Prince gave her his stepmother's message and the second largest ring. The giantess was greatly pleased when she saw the ring, and at once challenged Sigurd to wrestle with her.

They struggled for a long time, till at last Sigurd grew faint; so she handed him a horn to drink from, and when he had drunk he became so strong that he threw her down with one hand.

On the third morning Sigurd once more laid down his ball, and it rolled far away, till at last it stopped under a very high rock indeed, over the top of which the most hideous giantess that ever was seen looked down.

When she saw who was there she cried out: "Ah, this is just what I wanted! Here comes Prince Sigurd. Into the pot he goes this very night. Come up here, my friend, and wrestle with me." And she hauled him up just as her sisters had done.

Sigurd then gave her his stepmother's message and the last and largest ring. The sight of the red gold delighted the giantess, and she challenged Sigurd to a wrestling match. This time the fight was fierce and long, but when at length Sigurd's strength was failing the giantess gave him something to drink, and after he had drunk it he soon brought her to her knees, and was cured.

"You have beaten me," she gasped, "so now, listen to me. Not far from here is a lake. Go there and you will find a girl playing with a boat. Try to make friends with her, and give her this little

The Most Hideous Giantess that Ever was Seen

gold ring. You are stronger than ever you were, and I wish you good luck."

With these words they took leave of each other, and Sigurd wandered on till he reached the lake, where he found the girl playing with a boat, just as he had been told. He went up to her and asked what her name was.

She was called Helga, she answered, and she lived near by.

So Sigurd gave her the little gold ring, and proposed that they should have a game. The girl was delighted, for she had no brothers or sisters, and they played together all the rest of the day.

When evening came Sigurd asked leave to go home with her, but Helga at first forbade him, as no stranger had ever managed to enter their house without being found out by her father, who was a very fierce giant.

However, Sigurd persisted, and at length she gave way; but when they came near the door she held her glove over him and Sigurd was at once transformed into a bundle of wool. Helga tucked the bundle under her arm and threw it in her room.

Almost at the same moment her father rushed in and hunted round in every corner, crying out: "This place smells of men. What's that you threw on the bed, Helga?"

"A bundle of wool," said she.

"Oh well, perhaps it was that I smelt," said the old man, and troubled himself no more.

The following day Helga went out to play and took the bun-

Sigurd Found the Girl.

dle of wool with her under her arm. When she reached the lake she held her glove over it again and Sigurd resumed his own shape.

They played the whole day, and Sigurd taught Helga all sorts of games she had never even heard of. As they walked home in the evening she said: "We shall be able to play better still to-morrow, for my father will have to go to town, so we can stay at home."

When they were near the house Helga again held her glove over Sigurd, and once more he was turned into a bundle of wool, and she carried him in without his being seen.

Very early the next morning Helga's father went to town, and as soon as he was well out of the way the girl held up her glove and Sigurd was himself again. Then she took him all over the house to amuse him, and opened every room, for her father had given her the keys before he left; but when they came to the last room Sigurd noticed one key on the bunch which had not been used and asked which room it belonged to.

Helga grew red and did not answer.

"I suppose you don't mind my seeing the room which it opens?" asked Sigurd, and as he spoke he saw a heavy iron door and begged Helga to unlock it for him. But she told him she dared not do so, at least if she *did* open the door it must only be a *very* tiny chink; and Sigurd declared that would do quite well.

The door was so heavy that it took Helga some time to open it, and Sigurd grew so impatient that he pushed it wide open and walked in. There he saw a splendid horse, all ready and saddled,

A Bundle of Wool

and just above it hung a richly ornamented sword on the handle of which was engraved these words: "He who rides this horse and wears this sword will find happiness."

At the sight of the horse Sigurd was so filled with wonder that he was not able to speak, but at last he gasped out: "Oh, do let me mount him and ride him round the house! Just once; I promise not to ask any more."

"Ride him round the house!" cried Helga, growing pale at the mere idea. "Ride Gullfaxi! Why, father would never, *never* forgive me, if I let you do that."

"But it can't do him any harm," argued Sigurd; "you don't know *how* careful I will be. I have ridden all sorts of horses at home, and have never fallen off — not *once*. Oh, Helga, do!"

"Well, perhaps, if you come back *directly*," replied Helga, doubtfully; "but you must be very quick, or father will find out!"

But, instead of mounting Gullfaxi, as she expected, Sigurd stood still.

"And the sword," he said, looking fondly up to the place where it hung. "My father is a King, but he has not got any sword so beautiful as that. Why, the jewels in the scabbard are more splendid than the big ruby in his crown! Has it got a name? Some swords have, you know."

"It is called the Battle Plume," answered Helga, "and Gullfaxi means Golden Mane. I don't suppose, if you *are* to get on the horse at all, it would matter your taking the sword, too. And if you take

"Ride Gallfaxi! Never, *Never!*"

the sword, you will have to carry the stick and the stone and the twig as well."

"They are easily carried," said Sigurd, gazing at them with scorn. "What wretched dried-up things! Why in the world do you keep them?"

"Father says that he would rather lose Gullfaxi than lose them," replied Helga, "for if the man who rides the horse is pursued, he has only to throw the twig behind him and it will turn into a forest, so thick that even a bird could hardly fly through. But if his enemy knows magic, and can throw down the forest, the man has only to strike the stone with the stick, and hailstones as large as pigeons' eggs will rain down from the sky for twenty miles round."

Having said all this she allowed Sigurd to ride "just once" round the house, taking the sword and other things with him. But when he had ridden round, instead of dismounting, he suddenly turned the horse's head and galloped away.

Soon after this Helga's father came home and found his daughter in tears. He asked what was the matter, and when he heard all that had happened, he rushed off as fast as he could to pursue Sigurd.

Now, as Sigurd looked behind him, he saw the giant coming after him with great strides, and in all haste he threw the twig behind him. Immediately such a thick wood sprang up between him and his enemy that the giant was obliged to run home for an ax with which to cut his way through.

He Suddenly Turned the Horse's Head.

The next time Sigurd glanced round, the giant was so near that he almost touched Gullfaxi's tail. In an agony of fear Sigurd turned quickly in his saddle and hit the stone with the stick. No sooner had he done this than a terrible hailstorm burst behind, and the giant was killed on the spot.

After the giant was dead, Sigurd rode on towards his own home, and on the way he suddenly met his stepmother's little dog, running to meet him, with tears pouring down its face. He galloped on as hard as he could, and on arriving found nine menservants in the act of tying Queen Ingiborg to a post in the courtyard of the palace, where they intended to burn her.

Wild with anger, Prince Sigurd sprang from his horse and, sword in hand, fell on the men. Then he released his stepmother, and went in with her to see his father.

The King lay in bed sick with sorrow, neither eating nor drinking, for he thought that his son had been killed by the Queen. He could hardly believe his own eyes for joy when he saw the Prince, and Sigurd told him all his adventures.

After that Prince Sigurd rode back to fetch Helga, and a great feast was made which lasted three days; and every one said no bride was ever seen so beautiful as Helga, and they lived happily for many, many years, and everybody loved them.

He Released His Stepmother.

Firm and Straight on That One Leg

THE · CONSTANT · TIN · SOLDIER

By Hans Christian Andersen

O nce upon a time a lucky little boy was given a set of beautiful matched tin soldiers. There were twenty-five of them, all fitted neatly in their box. They had been made from the same piece of metal, so they were all exactly the same: they stood at attention, their guns at the ready, their uniforms of purple trimmed with gold, shiny and new. All exactly alike, yes; except for the very last one. There was not quite enough of the tin to make him complete, and thus he had only one leg. But he stood as firm and straight on that one leg as did all the other, complete soldiers on two. It is this last tin soldier that the story is about.

After the little boy had played happily with the soldiers for a long time, he placed them on a table with his other favorite toys and went off to bed.

There were many different kinds of toys there already, but the most remarkable one was a majestic castle. It was made of sturdy paperboard. Through the windows you could see straight into the lovely decorated rooms inside. Toy trees had been placed around the castle, and in front of it a small round mirror looked like a shining lake. Wax swans were set on the lake, as though they were swimming, and the effect was very real and marvelous.

But most beautiful of all was a little paper doll, who stood at the open door of the castle. She wore a dress of gauze, and a violet ribbon like a scarf over her shoulders, and clasping the scarf was an enormous shining silver tinsel rose. The paper doll was a dancer, and had her arms stretched out, and one leg lifted high as she balanced on the other.

The tin soldier could not see this leg lifted perfectly straight in the air, and thought that, like himself, the dancer had only one leg.

"What a wonderful wife she would make me!" the tin soldier thought. "Although she seems so far above me, living in a castle as she does, while I make my home in a box, and with twenty-four other soldiers at that. That would not be the place for her, but I must try to meet her nevertheless."

He lay down full length behind the wooden box which lay on the table. From there he could easily watch the dancer, as she continued to stand on one leg without losing her balance.

Soon it was night, and all of the people in the house now went to bed. This was the time when the toys themselves came

Most Beautiful Toy of All

out to play. The other soldiers wanted to join in, but they had been put back in the tin box, and could not move. But from his place behind the wooden box, our tin soldier could see everything.

The nutcracker turned somersaults while a mechanical pencil drew and doodled on the table. The canary bird in its cage began to sing. All of the toys became very active, speaking and playing according to their natures. The only two who did not stir were the tin soldier and the paper dancer. She still stood on one leg without losing her balance; and he was just as constant in his way, never taking his eyes off her.

The clock struck twelve and the lid flew off the wooden box; there was nothing in it, but a little goblin.

"Tin soldier," said the goblin, "don't stare at things that don't concern you."

The tin soldier pretended not to hear him.

"Just you wait till tomorrow!" said the goblin.

When the morning came, the children got up, the tin soldier was placed in the window, and whether it was the goblin or the draft that did it, all at once the window flew open, and the soldier fell, head over heels, out of the third story. That was a terrible fright! He put his leg straight up, and hit with his helmet downward, and his bayonet between the paving-stones.

The little boy came down to look for him, but though he almost stepped on him, he could not see him. If the soldier cried

The Toys Came Out to Play.

out, "Here I am!" he would have found him; but the soldier did not think it fitting to call out, because he was in uniform.

It began to rain; the drops soon fell thicker, and at last it came down in a complete stream. When the rain was past, two boys came by.

"Just look!" said one of them. "There lies a tin soldier. He must come out and ride in the boat."

And they made a boat out of a newspaper, and put the tin soldier in the middle of it; he sailed down the gutter, and the two boys ran beside him and clapped their hands. How the waves rose in that gutter, and how fast the stream ran! But it had been a heavy rain. The paper boat rocked up and down, and sometimes turned round so rapidly that the tin soldier trembled; but he remained firm, and never changed expression, but looked straight ahead, shouldering his gun.

All at once the boat went into a long drain, and it became as dark as if he had been in his box.

"Where am I going now?" he thought. "It's all the goblin's fault. Ah! If the little dancer only sat here with me in the boat, it might be twice as dark for all I would care."

Suddenly there came a great water rat, which lived under the drain.

"Have you a passport?" asked the rat. "Give me your passport."

But the tin soldier kept silent, and held his gun tighter than ever.

They Made a Boat Out of Newspaper.

The boat went on, but the rat came after it. He gnashed his teeth, and called out to the bits of straw and wood, "Hold him! Hold him! He hasn't paid a toll — he hasn't shown his passport!"

But the stream became stronger and stronger. The tin soldier could see daylight where the arch ended, but he heard a roaring noise, which might well frighten a bolder man. Just where the tunnel ended, the drain ran into a great canal; and for him, that was as dangerous as for us to be carried down a great waterfall.

Now he was already so near it that he could not stop. The boat was carried out, the poor tin soldier stiffened himself as much as he could, and never did he move an eyelid. The boat whirled round three or four times, and was full of water to the very edge.

The tin soldier stood up to his neck in water, the boat sank deeper and deeper, and the paper was loosened more and more; and now the water closed over the soldier's head. Then he thought of the pretty little dancer, and how he would never see her again.

And now the paper boat fell apart, and the tin soldier fell out; but at that very moment he was snapped up by a great fish.

Oh, how dark it was in that fish's body! It was darker even than in the drain tunnel, and it was very narrow, too. But the tin soldier remained, at full length, shouldering his gun.

The fish swam to and fro; he made the most wonderful movements, and then became quite still. At last something flashed through him like lightning.

The daylight shone quite clear, and a voice said aloud, "The

"He Hasn't Shown His Passport!"

tin soldier!" The fish had been caught, carried to market, bought, and taken into the kitchen, where the cook cut him open with a large knife. She seized the soldier round the body with both her hands, and carried him into the room, where all were anxious to see the remarkable man who had traveled about in the inside of a fish.

They placed him on the table and there — the tin soldier was in the very room in which he had been before! He saw the same children, and the same toys stood upon the table; and there was the pretty castle with the graceful little dancer. She was still balancing herself on one leg, and held the other extended in the air. She was faithful, too.

That moved the tin soldier; he was very near weeping tin tears, but that would not have been proper. He looked at her, but they said nothing to each other.

Then one of the little boys took the tin soldier, and flung him into the stove, for no reason. It must have been the work of the goblin in the box.

The tin soldier stood there all illuminated, and felt a heat that was terrible; but whether this heat proceeded from the real fire or from love he did not know. The color had left him; but whether that had happened on the journey, or had been caused by grief, no one could say. He looked at the little lady, she looked at him, and he felt that he was melting; but he stood firm, shouldering his gun.

Then suddenly the door flew open, and the draft of air caught

The Very Same Room!

the dancer, and she flew like a bird into the stove to the tin soldier, and flashed up in a flame, and then was gone!

The tin soldier melted down into a lump, and when the servant took out the ashes next day, she found him in the shape of a little tin heart. Of the dancer nothing remained but the silver tinsel rose, and that was burned as black as coal.

Nothing Remained . . .

Prince Toringarde

Everything to Make Him Happy

THE · PRINCESS ·
AND · THE · PEA

O nce upon a time there lived a handsome young Prince named Toringarde. He was beloved by all his subjects; the King and Queen, his father and mother doted on him entirely. Toringarde had everything to make him happy, yet happy he was not.

Toringarde longed to be in love. There were exactly fourteen Princesses in nearby kingdoms who longed for Prince Toringarde to be in love with them, and the Queen wept daily because her son would have none of them.

"No, mother," said Toringarde at least once a day, "no one will I marry who is not a real princess."

"But there are fourteen," his mother would remind him. "Fourteen fair ladies to choose from!"

"I will have none but a real princess," Toringarde would repeat. "And I don't believe in any of those."

And so it went. His father pleaded and his mother begged. The fourteen fathers of the fourteen Princesses sent ambassadors and emissaries; they proposed alliances and they threatened wars, but not one of them could prevail. Prince Toringarde still could find no bride.

There came a night so stormy and wild that the wind whistled around the turrets and blew down the banners and pennants. The rain fell so hard that the moat filled to overflowing. Sleet and hail pelted the thick stone walls, and the very chains and swords rattled and creaked in their casings.

It was so noisy, in fact, that it took a long time for anyone inside to hear the knocking at the castle door. All the court was huddled around the giant fireplace when suddenly the King said, "I hear someone at the door."

Immediately everyone fell silent, trying to listen between the howling of the wind and beating of the rain.

"I hear it now. Who can it be, on so wild a night?" said the Queen.

"I will go and see," said Prince Toringarde, hand on his sword.

"No," said the King, from his high seat, "I will go myself."

All the court waited fearfully for his return. Moments later, the King came in, bringing with him a creature so wet, so bedraggled, so torn by the storm that it was hard to see that she was a beautiful young maiden, a Princess indeed, as so she introduced herself as she sat under the many blankets that the servants ran to fetch.

"I am Princess Annasara," she announced. "I thank you for your hospitality and wish for a bed and shelter for the night. I am a long way from home."

"I Am Princess Annasara."

Everyone leaned forward to hear her story of getting lost in the dreadful storm. As she spoke, and the color came back to her cheeks, Prince Toringarde thought he had never seen anyone half as lovely. And as Princess Annasara told her tale, he thought he had never listened to anyone as charming. This, he told himself, must be the true Princess he had always waited for.

As the court prepared to retire, Prince Toringarde took his mother aside. "I love Princess Annasara," he declared. "But if she be not a real Princess, then I will be alone and unhappy forever."

"Leave it to me, my son," the Queen declared. "Only a Princess of Princesses can pass my test."

With that, the Queen went to the bedroom of their unexpected guest. She put a tiny green pea beneath the mattress, and then piled on top of them twenty layers of mattresses, blankets, sheets, and still more mattresses till they nearly towered to the ceiling.

Princess Annasara murmured her thanks as she climbed up. She lay herself down on the topmost mattress to sleep.

In the morning, everyone awaited the Princess, but none more so than the Queen and Prince, who bowed low as the Princess entered the room where all were assembled.

"Good morning, my dear," the King greeted her. "I hope you have slept well."

Princess Annasara curtsied before him. "Oh your majesty," she replied, "I do appreciate the kindness you have shown me, and do not wish to appear ungrateful, but — " She blushed as she spoke.

Nearly to the Ceiling

"What is it, my dear?" inquired the Queen. "Did you not have a good night's sleep?"

"Oh majesty," Princess Annasara wailed, "I would have slept very beautifully indeed, but the bed was so uncomfortable. There was something so hard in it that I was totally unable to sleep, and have been bruised black and blue with twisting and turning on it."

"My dear!" exclaimed the Queen, beaming broadly and throwing her arms around Annasara. "My dear, dear Princess!"

Now Prince Toringarde stepped forward. The Queen took one of his hands and joined it with that of the Princess, smiling happily at both of them.

"Now what's all this?" the King asked gruffly. "What's going on here? I don't understand!"

"You will, my dearest," the Queen promised. She turned to Annasara. "My son Toringarde will have only a true princess for his wife. Last night, I put the tiniest green pea on the bed, and covered it with twenty layers of mattresses and blankets. Now, only a true princess could be so delicate as to feel that pea and be unable to sleep because of it!"

"You are my true Princess, and my true love," declared Prince Toringarde. "A lucky storm brought you to our kingdom, and here you will stay by my side for ever and ever!"

And so it was. Before the springtime, when the tiny green peas in their pods burst through the soil again, the marriage of Annasara and Toringarde was celebrated in the two kingdoms.

"Only a True Princess Could Be So Delicate!"

Bits and Pieces from the Villagers

DICK · WHITTINGTON · AND · HIS · CAT

O nce upon a time in a small village in England there lived a small boy named Dick Whittington. His father and mother had died when he was just a baby, and the poor, ragged orphan lived on what bits and pieces the villagers gave him. This was not very much at all, for the place itself was very poor and there was little enough to spare for a boy who belonged to nobody.

Now Dick may have been very poor, but he was also a very bright, intelligent boy. He paid close attention to everything that was going on, and he stored away every piece of information he received as if it was something precious indeed.

People in those days, especially in out of the way places like Dick's village, had very little to amuse them besides the conversation and company they provided for each other and for themselves. So Dick would listen in to the farmers' talk, when they came to the village for market days. You may be sure he also paid sharp attention to the clergyman's sermons every Sunday, and day in, day out, in all the little stores and shops of the village, Dick listened.

DICK WHITTINGTON AND HIS CAT

Of all the places and things he heard about, none stirred his imagination so much as talk about the great city of London, capital of all England, and to Dick's young mind, the very center of all the universe. For surely there could be no place in the world so rich, so splendid, so important, as the great London he was always hearing about.

Folks spoke about it as though the very streets were paved with gold, there for the taking, and opportunity for everyone who tried to become fine lords and ladies of the great city itself.

Of all the dreams and desires that filled the mind and stirred the imagination of young Dick Whittington, none was so strong as the thought that he himself might one day go up to Londontown.

Several years had passed this way, and Dick was a boy in his teens. As he was now old enough and strong enough, he worked whenever he could around the courtyard and stables of the village inn, thus earning his bread. In those days, inns were the center of activity for any village; all traffic and travel being by stagecoach or on horseback, an inn was the destination of every traveler. Thus they were busy places, with much coming and going, and much to be done in the way of caring for the horses, the coaches, and the passengers who came either to refresh themselves at table or stay overnight.

The times that Dick loved best were when large coaches, pulled by teams of horses and filled with passengers, came to a halt at the inn. Then there was sure to be plenty of hurrying and scur-

Old Enough and Strong Enough

rying, plenty of work to be done, and perhaps even an extra tip or two for a boy who managed to give good service.

Beyond that, it was the best chance of all to hear news of the outside world, and learn what was happening out far beyond the horizons of the little village.

It was just at such a time, that a large coach, drawn by a team of eight lively horses, drew up to the courtyard of the inn.

The coachman was a fine, tall fellow, and when the stableman had seen to his horses, he called loudly for a tankard for himself.

None in attendance were so quick as Dick Whittington to answer such a call. "Here you are, sir," he said, holding the foaming tankard up to where the coachman sat on his high seat.

"Thank you, my lad, thank you," roared the coachman. "I dare say you're the liveliest boy on all the King's highway for bringing a man his drink when it's needed!"

Dick's eyes shone at the unaccustomed praise. He stood by, waiting while the coachman downed his draft and made ready to descend.

The paying passengers had made their way to the inn's dining room, but Dick followed the coachman to the kitchen, where all those men of the road customarily ate. The boy stayed in the shadows, not putting himself forward, but listening to all the talk at table, his sharp ears missing nothing.

As he supposed, the coach was on its way to London, and had only stopped so that the passengers might refresh themselves while

"Here You Are, Sir."

the horses were being changed.

After the hardy coachman had eaten and drunk his fill, he made ready to get underway again. Dick followed him out, and this time he moved and spoke quickly.

"Please sir," he said, "I want more than anything to go to London. Please sir, could you take me with you?"

The coachman laughed heartily, throwing back his head, his long dark hair shaking. "So you've heard about the gold in the streets of London, have you, boy?" he asked.

"Yes sir, please sir," Dick replied. "And I'll be all the help that I can along the way. I'll see to the horses, and attend the passengers, and do whatever you need me to do!"

"There's many a less likely lad than you that's made his way to Londontown, and found his fortune," the coachman replied, looking keenly at Dick. "Come along then, and let's see if the city makes a man of you as well!"

Dick was ecstatic. There was no room inside the coach with the paying passengers, of course, and while Dick would have loved to have shared the high outside seat with the coachman, that was taken as well. There was nothing but for him to perch on the little seat set in the back of the coach, his hands clutching the sides for dear life, his feet dangling just inches above the mud and stones thrown up by the horses' hooves and the racing wheels of the coach. It meant that he was facing backwards, seeing what they had already passed, rather than looking forward. But for a boy who

"I Want to Go to London."

had never set twenty steps outside of his own village, it was a rare treat indeed, and Dick never for a moment thought any the worse of his fine ride.

It was a journey of three days and three nights from the village to London, a far journey indeed in those times. That the wind went whistling through his thin shirt, even as the sharp little stones of the road scratched and cut his bare legs, was no bother to Dick in the least. He was off on the journey of his life, and the fascination of the road more than made up for any of its discomforts.

He walked hard and cheerfully as the coachman directed, jumping from his seat at each village and town even before the horses had completely halted. Thus did he earn a couple of pennies along the way, although it would be much said in later years that Dick Whittington had arrived in London with not a cent in his ragged empty pockets.

At last they reached the outskirts of the great city. So many streets! So many buildings! There were so many people and carriages, animals and wagons, everything going in such great numbers and equally great haste that poor Dick Whittington, hugging his perch on the back of the coach, did not have eyes enough to go all around to see all the sights there were to see.

He felt the tall buildings as though they were closing in on him, and the ramble of streets was such a maze he thought he would never be able to find his way in or out, and he marveled that the coachman could steer them so steadily onward, seeming-

The Journey of His Life

ly never losing his way until all of the passengers had at last disembarked. The coach came to a halt. Dick jumped from his seat.

"Well, my fine young fellow," called the merry coachman as he threw the reins down to Dick, "what do you think of fine Londontown now?"

Dick scarcely knew what to answer. All along the streets they had ridden he had seen cobblestones, mud, dirt, and other things more familiar to a country lad. But of gold he had seen none, and he was anxious to get to where it was.

But walk though he would everywhere, and search high and low, Dick Whittington found no such streets. Even in the neighborhoods where the houses were large and fine, set back from the road and with beautiful gardens around them, the streets and roads were mostly mud, and even where they had been paved, it was with the commonest sort of brick or cobblestone. Of gold there was none.

Dick's few pennies did not go very far. He had to ask for half pennies from likely looking people in the street, so that he could get himself a bit of food, which seemed to him to cost ever so much more up in town than it ever had in the country, as meager as his fare had been there.

At last, quite worn out with looking and faint from hunger, he slid to the ground on the doorstep of the mansion of a wealthy merchant.

"Here! Take that! Away with you, lazy boy!" The cook of the

Of Gold There was None.

house came running out, striking and jabbing at Dick every which way with the stick of her broom. "Away with you! We don't want your filthy sort around here!"

Poor Dick struggled up, trying weakly to defend himself, his hands in front of his face to ward off the worst of the blows.

And just as he was getting the worst of it, a fine, prosperous looking gentleman came walking up. "Why cook," he exclaimed, "what is all this about?"

"This lazy, dirty good for nothing has chosen your doorstep sir, to partake himself a nap," the cook said. "And I was just beating him off for you, sir."

"I can see that, cook," the gentleman said, "but perhaps it may be that this boy is not quite as dangerous to the property as your blows would make him out to be." He looked down at Dick, who was still kneeling and trying to shield himself from the cook's broom.

"Please sir, I didn't mean any harm," Dick cried. "I didn't mean harm to your property, sir. It's just that I fell down — "

"Fell down!" the gentleman interrupted, echoing his words. "I pray sir, are you drunk?"

"Oh no," Dick said, summoning the last of his strength to defend himself against such a charge. "I do not drink, sir. Of late," and he lowered his voice still more, "of late, I have not had very much to eat either, sir. That is why I am in such a weakened state."

"You look old enough and strong enough to work," the gen-

"What is All This About?"

tleman said, looking at Dick far more kindly than the cook had. "Why don't you get some work and earn your bread?"

"If only I could, sir!" cried Dick. "That is what I have come all the way from home to try to do. But there doesn't seem to be much work for a poor boy like me."

"Perhaps you have come to the very right house after all," the gentleman said slowly. "Cook, you're always complaining of no one to help you with the dirty, heavy work of the kitchen. Let's give this poor lad a chance and see what he can do."

"Oh thank you, thank you, sir!" Dick exclaimed, trying to grab the gentleman's hand in gratitude.

"Here! None of that!" the cook said, using her toe none to gently to separate Dick from the gentleman. "You just come along with me and we'll see if you're worth the bother."

Dick pulled himself up, holding on to the solid stone wall of the house as he followed cook downstairs into a large kitchen. The fragrances from the various foods that were cooking and stewing nearly overwhelmed him.

Almost fainting again, he pulled himself into a chair, and laid his head on the table.

The cook scowled. "Already making himself at home, the common thing!" she said. "Here, get your filthy head off my clean table."

But even she could see that Dick had barely the strength to move. Grudgingly, she went to the stove and ladled some soup

"Let's Give This Poor Lad a Chance."

into a little bowl. "Here," she said, shoving it across the table to him, "have some of that. Then we'll put you to work."

Even though it was not offered kindly, Dick was nonetheless grateful. He ate the soup quickly, and felt his strength reviving.

He thanked the cook, and told her he was ready to do her bidding at once.

As he was getting three plain but hearty meals every day, all of his strength quickly returned and Dick became his usual cheerful self. He followed the cook's orders obediently, hauling and scouring the heavy black pots and kettles, taking the garbage out to be dumped, bringing in heavy armloads of wood to keep the fires in the stoves going, and any other heavy, dirty chores the cook could find for him. But Dick didn't mind the hard work at all. Except for the cook, it was a pleasant household; the other servants were kind to him, and having a warm place to sleep and good hot food to eat was as much as Dick would hope for.

One of Dick's closest friends in the house was a man far removed from him in age and station. He was Fitzwilliam the butler, who very much ran the house for Mr. Doverfield, the merchant. Fitzwilliam, as befit his position, was a very grand personage, and at first Dick had been a little afraid of him; but it turned out that Fitzwilliam had once had a son of his own, who had died at about the same age as Dick, and so he had a kindly feeling toward the boy.

Moreover, Fitzwilliam was possessed of a grand voice, and he loved nothing so much as to read aloud to the admiration of the

Dick didn't Mind the Hard Work at All.

other servants after their chores and duties were finished in the evenings. Within a short time, Dick became the most appreciative member of the butler's audience. He loved to hear the stories over and over again, finding that there was something to be learned from each of them, whether they were true histories or fantastic tales of a writer's imagination.

As Dick listened and learned and did his chores, he became more at home in the household. He was neat and clean now, particularly tidy about his person, and would never have been taken for the raggedy little urchin who had almost fainted on Mr. Doverfield's doorstep that day. That gentleman indeed was very proud of his own good judgment in securing Dick for the household, rather than leaving him to the streets. He took an interest in the boy, as much as was possible for a gentleman whose business kept him so occupied most of the time. Little by little, other chores and duties were found for Dick, for everyone in the household, family and servants alike, recognized his cleverness and were eager to use it to advantage.

Even Miss Louisa, Mr. Doverfield's daughter and only child, made rather a pet of Dick. Before long, he was given a good suit of clothes so that when either of the Doverfields or all of them went to church of a Sunday, Dick was properly attired to follow them, so that they, especially Miss Louisa, did not go out into the streets unattended.

From time to time he performed other little services for Miss

The Butler's Audience

Louisa, once rescuing her pet parrot when it flew out of the window and landed on a high branch of a tree that no one but Dick was capable of climbing. At another time, doing a bit of charity, Miss Louisa managed to drop her purseful of gold coins; had not Dick seen it on the street and quickly brought it to her, it might have been lost forever.

There was only one thing that kept Dick from being perfectly content with his position in the Doverfield house. He had a little room of his own, tiny and slopewalled, since it was set into the pitch of the roof, but all his own, and he was glad enough to have it, or would have been, were it not for the uninvited companions who shared it with him — a very flock of rats and mice that tumbled and squeaked about as if the room was theirs, and not his.

They made his life a very nuisance, keeping him from the sleep he needed so much after his hard day's work.

It happened one day that Mr. Doverfield had a visitor, another gentleman; Dick took such particular care of the visitor's needs that he was generously rewarded with several coins. Dick knew at once what he would do with this windfall.

He walked the streets up and down till he found an old woman with a cat. As she had several more at home, she was as willing to part with this one as Dick was with his coins. So the bargain was struck, and Dick tucked the cat under his arm, and brought her back to his little garret room.

As the old woman had promised, the cat was an excellent

Uninvited Companions

mouser, and within a very few weeks, Dick's room was as rid of the rats and mice as if they had never been there in the first place.

Soon after came a great event for the entire household. Mr. Doverfield, being a very considerate employer and always liking to see his people do well, called all of the servants into a small drawing room one evening after dinner. There he explained that he had undertaken the enterprise of sending a sailing ship to trade on the north coast of Africa. It would be an excellent opportunity for each of them to send whatever he or she had that they thought could be sold to the people there. Then each of them would get the profit of such a sale. All of them were excited at the opportunity to increase their meager earnings, and immediately began talking amongst themselves as to what they would send. It seemed as if everyone had something to give to the venture except Dick, whose little earnings had gone for candy and such, and whose only possession was his cat.

But he was determined to play his part, and to have something that he too could send along, and be able to discuss his chances of success with the other servants. So sadly, Dick decided to send away his cat. For you may be sure that this venture in which they were all partaking formed the greatest amount of interest possible among the servants, who could talk of little else from the time that the proposal had first been made to them.

Dick had tears in his eyes when he delivered her to the Captain of the sailing vessel, for she had proven her worth not only as

Sadly Sending Away His Cat

mouser but as companion, and he feared he would miss her on both counts.

At this, Miss Louisa, who always took Dick's part, offered to give him some coins so that he might get himself another cat.

Although Dick had been with them for many years, the cook was meaner to him than ever she had been at the beginning of his stay. She was a very jealous creature, and could not stand it whenever Miss Louisa showed Dick any sort of kindness or attention. Now the cook teased him mercilessly for having sent the cat to sea.

So cruelly did the cook treat him that in spite of the kindnesses of everyone else, Dick at last thought he could bear no more and decided to run away, and seek his fortune elsewhere.

He walked as far as a little way outside the city, when he came to a fork in the road. Tired from walking, he sat down for a moment to decide which way to go. As he sat thinking, church bells nearby began to chime. They seemed to speak out to him:

"Turn back, Whittington,
Lord Mayor of London."

Dick couldn't believe his ears. Still, he felt sure of what he had heard. "Lord Mayor of London!" he thought to himself. "If I'm to be Lord Mayor of London, what do the cook's blows and curses matter to me?"

Back he went, and managed to slip inside the house and to his chores before the nasty cook had even realized that he was gone.

Mr. Doverfield's ship, with Dick's cat and all the other ser-

Turn Back, Whittington, the Bells Seemed To Say.

vants' trade goods aboard, was at sea for a long time. At last the winds blew them to landfall on the Barbary Coast. Neither the people living there nor the Englishmen on the ship had ever seen each other's like before, so there was a great deal of interest and curiosity between them. At last, when the feelings of strangeness were overcome, the local people were very glad of the chance to buy the goods that filled the ship.

When the Captain saw that a great deal of good trading was very likely, he gathered up the best quality of everything on board and had it sent to the Barbary King.

So pleased was His Royal Majesty with these unexpected goods, that he had the Captain and other officers to the palace for a grand dinner.

Everything there was of a greater magnificence than anything these Englishmen had seen at home. They marvelled at the tapestries, the rich weavings, the vessels of gold and silver and finest glass that were everywhere. There were also endless lines of servants, magnificently outfitted, ready to serve the King's guests, and do all of his royal bidding.

But as soon as the Captain and the other guests were seated, and looking eagerly at the rich variety of dishes being placed before them, a veritable army of rats and mice jumped up everywhere, scurrying across the table, and helping themselves to food from every dish.

The Captain was amazed. "Begging your pardon, Your High-

A Greater Magnificence than Anything at Home

ness," he said, "do you not find these vermin most unpleasant?"

"Indeed I do!" exclaimed the King, while the Queen indica-
ted her displeasure and unhappiness at the condition of her dining
salon. "I would give half of my riches to be rid of them," the King
went on, "only we have not the means to do so."

"But we have, Your Highness," the Captain said, a gleam in
his eyes.

"Indeed!" said the King again. "Rid me of these pests, good
sir, and half the belongings of this palace are yours!"

The Captain wasted no time in sending a sailor to fetch
Dick's cat and bring her to the palace.

"Of course, this creature is a great pet of mine," the captain
said, "and there's very little which could cause me to part with
her."

"Very little is not what I had in mind," the King replied. "If
this creature is indeed able to rid me of this nuisance, everything I
promised in return will be given."

Well, a palace, even on the Barbary Coast, is bigger than a
garret by far, and it took the cat a while longer to clear things for
the King than it had to perform the same service for Dick. But at
last it was done, and the palace could function as a royal habitation
once more.

So impressed were their royal majesties, that they were not
only willing to give up half their household treasure for the cat's
performance, but offered up even more riches in return for keep-

"Rid Me of These Pests, Good Sir!"

ing her. All this the captain readily agreed to, and after reloading the ship with so much treasure that her boards were groaning, they took their leave of that pleasant place and sailed home for England once more.

As soon as they got there, the Captain presented himself to Mr. Doverfield, and quickly gave accounting of the adventure that had befallen them. The trip was a great success, with money made for all involved, but none so much as for that person who owned the now royal cat of Barbary.

Mr. Doverfield was as good as his word, and better. Even though some of the people around him suggested that it was too much to reward a poor scullery lad with anywhere near the treasure that had been sent him, Mr. Doverfield insisted. "It was the lad's doing," he said, "and it is just as surely the lad's reward. Far be it from me to take anything which is not mine. It all belongs to Dick, and he will be a great man now."

Dick was sent for. He was in the kitchen, scouring pots as usual, and dirt and grease covered his hands and arms, and even his face where he had unthinkingly touched it. "I can't go to the master like this," he protested, when the other servants told him that Mr. Doverfield was waiting for him. "I must clean myself and dress properly first."

But Mr. Doverfield himself, impatient to let the lad know of his great good fortune would not wait. He insisted that Dick come into his room, and even set a great chair for him to sit in.

An Accounting of the Great Adventure

Dick himself could not believe that such a thing was happening, and he believed that the servants were teasing him and playing him a trick as they so often did.

But they insisted, and so did Mr. Doverfield.

"My boy," he began, "prepare yourself. You are to become one of the great men of London, with riches beyond your dreams."

Poor Dick could only stare at him and not say a word.

Then Mr. Doverfield explained how successful the voyage had been for all concerned, but none more so than Dick himself.

When the lad realized the extent of his good fortune, he insisted that Mr. Doverfield share it with him, as it had been his employer's kindness that had made the venture possible in the first place.

"No, no," Mr. Doverfield insisted. "It is all yours, and I only hope that you will make good use of it, Mr. Dick Whittington."

"Then, sir," Dick replied, emboldened at the manner in which his employer was addressing him, "Miss Louisa shall share in my good fortune, because she has always been the soul of kindness to me, and I do indeed worship her."

"Not a bit of it," Mr. Doverfield insisted. "My daughter's fortune is her own, as this is yours, and the good name of our house demands that none of us take from you what is rightfully yours."

While this discussion was going on, another entirely more suitable room than the garret was being prepared for Dick. Then

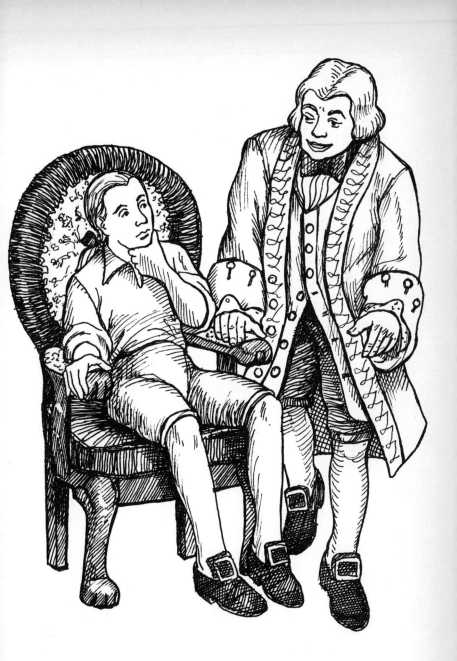

"My Boy, Prepare Yourself."

tailors, the finest in Londontown, were sent for so that he might be properly attired.

All this and more was done, and still there was more to his fortune than Dick supposed could ever be spent in one lifetime.

Although it had been forbidden to him to share his fortune with any of the family, he could not be prevented from making gifts of one sort or another to all of those who had been involved in his good fortune. He rewarded the Captain, the officers, and all of the sailors on the ship very liberally, and you may be sure that he remembered old Fitzwilliam and the other servants, even the nasty cook.

But he got the most pleasure from the trinkets and treasures he could present to Miss Louisa; for now that he was dressed and groomed as any wealthy young man of the town, it was found that he was as nice and as handsome, if not more so, than any of them. Much as Miss Louisa had favored him when he was only the poor scullery boy, now she was able to greet him from a position of greater equality than either of them would have ever dreamed possible.

As likely a lad as poor Dick had been, how much more interesting Miss Louisa found him now! So much so, that when he proposed marriage, she readily accepted; her father, Mr. Doverfield, as quickly and happily agreed to the match.

Now it can be told that Dick Whittington was a real person. He and Miss Louisa, now Mrs. Whittington, lived happily and

Making Gifts to All Involved

richly together for a long time. They were blessed with many children, who of course wanted for nothing, and who in turn, married into the greatest and most famous families in the land. Such was Dick Whittington's good deeds and fame throughout the kingdom that he even entertained the great King Henry the Fifth. At dinner the King toasted Dick Whittington, "Never has a King had such a subject." And Dick Whittington raised his goblet and said, "Never has a subject had such a King."

Upon hearing this gallantry, King Henry knighted the former scullery boy who was henceforward known as Sir Richard Whittington.

As such, he gave great sums to help the poor; built churches and hospitals; served his city and his country long and well, so much so that a statue of him, with his cat tucked under his arm, was carved in stone and set in a prominent square in London.

For a time he served as sheriff of the city, and several times, as the bells of Bow Church had proclaimed that day so long ago, was Dick Whittington Lord Mayor of London.

They Were Blessed with Many Children.

He Sewed for Dear Life.

THE · BRAVE · LITTLE · TAILOR

O ne summer's day a little tailor sat on his table by the window in the best of spirits and sewed for dear life. As he was sitting thus a peasant woman came down the street, calling out: "Good jam to sell! Good jam to sell!"

This sounded sweetly in the tailor's ears. He put his frail little head out of the window and shouted: "Up here, my good woman, and you'll find a willing customer."

The woman climbed up the three flights of stairs with her heavy basket to the tailor's room, and he made her spread out all the pots in a row before him. He examined them all, lifted them up and smelled them, and said at last: "This jam seems good. Weigh me four ounces of it, my good woman; and even if it's a quarter of a pound I won't stick at it."

The woman, who had hoped to make a good sale, gave him what he wanted, but went away grumbling wrathfully.

"Now Heaven shall bless this jam for my use," cried the little tailor, "and it shall sustain and strengthen me." He fetched some bread out of a cupboard, cut a round off the loaf, and spread the jam on it. "That won't taste amiss," he said; "but I'll finish that waistcoat first before I take a bite."

He placed the bread beside him, went on sewing, and out of the lightness of his heart kept on making his stitches bigger and bigger. In the meantime the smell of the sweet jam rose to the ceiling, where heaps of flies were sitting, and attracted them to such an extent that they swarmed on to it in masses.

"Ha! Who invited you?" asked the tailor, and chased the unwelcome guests away. But the flies, who didn't understand, refused to be warned off, and returned again in even greater numbers.

At last the little tailor, losing all patience, reached out to his chimney corner for a duster, and exclaiming, "Wait, and I'll give it to you," he beat them mercilessly with it. When he left off he counted the slain, and no fewer than seven lay dead before him with outstretched legs.

"What a brave fellow I am!" said he, and was filled with admiration at his own courage. "The whole town must know about this." And in great haste the little tailor cut out a wide belt, hemmed it, and embroidered on it in big letters, "Seven at one blow."

"What did I say, the town? No, the whole world shall hear of it," he said; and his heart beat for joy as a lamb wags its tail.

The tailor strapped the belt round his waist and set out into the wide world, for he considered his workroom too small a field for his prowess. Before he set forth he looked round about him, to

"Who Invited You?"

see if there was anything in the house he could take with him on his journey; but he found nothing except an old cheese, which he took.

In front of the house he observed a bird that had been caught in some bushes, and this he put into his pack beside the cheese. Then he went on his way merrily, and being light and agile he never felt tired.

His way led up a hill, on the top of which sat a powerful giant, who was calmly surveying the landscape.

The little tailor went up to him, and greeting him cheerfully said: "Good day, friend, here you sit at your ease viewing the whole wide world. I'm just on my way there. What do you say to accompanying me?"

The giant looked contemptuously at the tailor and said: "What a poor wretched little creature you are!"

"That's a good joke," answered the little tailor, and unbuttoning his coat he showed the giant the belt. "There now, you can read what sort of a fellow I am."

The giant read, "Seven at one blow," and thinking they were human beings the tailor had slain, he conceived a certain respect for the little man. But first he thought he'd test him, so taking up a stone in his hand he squeezed it till some drops of water ran out. "Now you do the same," said the giant, "if you really wish to be thought strong."

"Is that all?" said the little tailor, "That's child's play to me."

"Seven At One Blow"

So he dived into his pack, brought out the cheese, and pressed it till the whey ran out. "My squeeze was in sooth better than yours," said he.

The giant didn't know what to say, for he couldn't have believed it of the little fellow. To prove him again, the giant lifted a stone and threw it so high that the eye could hardly follow it. "Now, my little pygmy, let me see you do that."

"Well thrown," said the tailor; "but, after all, your stone fell to the ground. I'll throw one that won't come down at all." He dived into his pack again, and grasping the bird in his hand, he threw it up into the air. The bird, enchanted to be free, soared up into the sky and flew away never to return.

"Well, what do you think of that little piece of business, friend?" asked the tailor.

"You can certainly throw," said the giant; "but now let's see if you can carry a proper weight." With these words he led the tailor to a huge oak tree which had been felled to the ground and said: "If you are strong enough, help me to carry the tree out of the wood."

"Most certainly," said the little tailor. "Just you take the trunk on your shoulder. I'll bear the top and branches, which is certainly the heaviest part." The giant laid the trunk on his shoulder, but the tailor sat at his ease among the branches; and the giant, who couldn't see what was going on behind him, had to carry the whole tree and the little tailor in the bargain. There he sat behind in the

"Let Me See You Do That."

best of spirits, lustily whistling a tune, as if carrying the tree were mere sport.

The giant, after dragging the heavy weight for some time, could get on no further and shouted out: "Hi! I must let the tree fall."

The tailor sprang nimbly down, seized the tree with both hands as if he had carried it the whole way, and said to the giant: "Fancy a big lout like you not being able to carry a tree!"

They continued to go on their way together, and as they passed by a cherry tree the giant grasped the top of it, where the ripest fruit hung, gave the branches into the tailor's hand, and bade him eat. But the little tailor was far too weak to hold the tree down, and when the giant let go, the tree swung back into the air, bearing the little tailor with it.

When he had fallen to the ground again without hurting himself, the giant said: "What! Do you mean to tell me you haven't the strength to hold down a feeble twig?"

"It wasn't strength that was wanting," replied the tailor. "Do you think that would have been anything for a man who has killed seven at one blow? I jumped over the tree because the huntsmen are shooting among the branches near us. Do the like if you dare."

The giant made an attempt, but couldn't get over the tree, and stuck fast in the branches, so that here too the little tailor had the better of him.

"Well, you're a fine fellow, after all," said the giant. "Come

The Tailor Sprang Nimbly Down.

and spend the night with us in our cave." The little tailor willingly consented to do this, and following his friend they went on till they reached a cave where several other giants were sitting round a fire, each holding a roast sheep, of which he was eating.

The little tailor looked about him and thought: "Yes, there's certainly more room to turn round in here than in my workshop." The giant showed him a bed and bade him lie down and have a good sleep. But the bed was too big for the little tailor, so he didn't get into it, but crept away into the corner.

At midnight, when the giant thought the little tailor was fast asleep, he rose up, and taking his big iron walking-stick, he broke the bed in two with a blow, and thought he had made an end of the little tailor.

At early dawn, the giants went off to the wood and quite forgot about the little tailor, till all of a sudden they met him trudging along in the most cheerful manner. The giants were terrified at the apparition, and, fearful lest he should slay them, they all took to their heels as fast as they could.

The little tailor continued to follow his nose, and after he had wandered about for a long time he came to the courtyard of a royal palace, and feeling tired he lay down on the grass and fell asleep.

While he lay there the people came, and looking him all over read on his belt: "Seven at one blow."

"Oh!" they said, "what can this great hero of a hundred fights want in our peaceful land? He must indeed be a mighty man of

More Room to Turn Around In

valor." They went and told the King about him, and said what a weighty and useful man he'd be in time of war, and that it would be well to secure him at any price.

This counsel pleased the King, and he sent one of his courtiers down to the little tailor, to offer him, when he awoke, a commission in their army. The messenger remained standing by the sleeper and waited till he stretched his limbs and opened his eyes, when the messenger tendered his proposal.

"That's the very thing I came here for," the tailor answered. "I am quite ready to enter the King's service." So he was received with all honor and given a special house of his own to live in.

But the other officers resented the success of the little tailor, and wished him a thousand miles away. "What's to come of it all?" they asked each other. "If we quarrel with him he'll let out at us, and at every blow seven will fall. There'll soon be an end of us."

So they resolved to go in a body to the King and to all send in their papers of resignation. "We are not made," they said, "to hold out against a man who kills seven at one blow."

The King was grieved at the thought of losing all his faithful servants for the sake of one man, and he wished heartily that he had never set eyes on the tailor, or that he could get rid of him. But the King didn't dare to send him away, for he feared he might kill him along with his people, and place himself on the throne. He pondered long and deeply over the matter and finally came to a conclusion.

"Quite Ready to Enter the King's Service"

THE BRAVE LITTLE TAILOR

He sent to the tailor and told him that, seeing what a great and warlike hero he was, he was about to make him an offer.

In a certain wood of his kingdom there dwelt two giants who did much harm by the way they robbed, murdered, burned, and plundered everything about them; no one could approach them without endangering his life. But if he could overcome and kill these two giants he should have the King's only daughter for a wife, and half his kingdom in the bargain; he might have a hundred horsemen, too, to back him up.

"That's the very thing for a man like me," thought the little tailor, "one doesn't get the offer of a beautiful Princess and half a kingdom every day."

"Done," he answered; "I'll soon put an end to the giants. But I haven't the smallest need of your hundred horsemen; a fellow who can slay seven men at one blow need not be afraid of two."

The little tailor set out and the hundred horsemen followed him. When he came to the outskirts of the wood he said to his followers: "You wait here, I'll manage the giants by myself." He went into the wood, casting his sharp little eyes right and left about him. After a while he spied the two giants lying asleep under a tree and snoring till the very boughs bent with the breeze.

The little tailor lost no time in filling his pack with stones, and then climbed up the tree under which they lay. When he got to the middle of it, he slipped along a branch till he sat just above the sleepers, when he threw down one stone after the other on the

About to Make Him an Offer

nearest giant.

The giant felt nothing for a long time, but at last he woke up, and pinching his companion said, "What did you strike me for?"

"I didn't strike you," said the other, "you must be dreaming."

They both lay down to sleep again, and the tailor threw down a stone on the second giant, who sprang up and cried: "What's that for? Why did you throw something at me?"

"I didn't throw anything," growled the first one. They wrangled on for a time, till, as both were tired, they made up and fell asleep again.

The little tailor began his game once more, and flung the largest stone he could find in his pack with all his force and hit the first giant on the chest. "This is too much of a good thing!" the giant yelled, and springing up like a madman, he knocked his companion against the tree till he trembled. He gave, however, as good as he got, and they became so enraged that they tore up trees and beat each other with them till they both fell at once on the ground.

Then the little tailor jumped down. "It's a mercy," he said, "that they didn't root up the tree on which I was perched, or I should have had to jump like a squirrel on to another, which, nimble though I am, would have been no easy job."

He drew his sword and gave each of the giants a thrust or two on the breast, and then went to the horsemen and said: "The deed is done. I've put an end to the two of them; but I assure you it has been no easy matter, for they even tore up trees in their struggle to

The Largest Stone He Could Find

defend themselves; but all that's of no use against one who slays seven men at one blow."

"Weren't you wounded?" asked the horsemen.

"No fear," answered the tailor. "They haven't touched a hair of my head." But the horsemen wouldn't believe him till they rode into the wood and found the giants and the trees lying around, torn up by the roots.

The little tailor now demanded the promised reward from the King, who repented his promise, and pondered once more how he could rid himself of the hero. "Before you obtain the hand of my daughter and half my kingdom," he said, "you must do another deed of valor. A unicorn is running about loose in the wood and doing much mischief. You must first catch it."

"I'm even less afraid of one unicorn than of two giants. Seven at one blow, that's my motto." He took a piece of cord and an ax with him, went out to the wood, and again told the men who had been sent with him to remain outside.

He hadn't to search long, for the unicorn soon passed by, and, perceiving the tailor, dashed straight at him as though it were going to spike him on the spot.

"Gently, gently," said he, "not so fast, my friend," and standing still he waited till the beast was quite near, when he sprang lightly behind a tree.

The unicorn ran with all its force against the tree, and rammed its horn so firmly into the trunk that it had no strength

"A Unicorn is Running About Loose."

left to pull it out again, and was thus successfully captured.

"Now I've caught my bird," said the tailor, and he came out from behind the tree, placed the cord round its neck, then struck the horn out of the tree with his ax, and, when everything was in order led the beast before the King.

Still the King didn't want to give him the promised reward, and made a third demand. The tailor was to catch a wild boar for him that did a great deal of harm in the wood, and he might have the huntsmen to help him.

"Willingly," said the tailor. "That's mere child's play." But he didn't take the huntsmen into the wood with him, and they were well enough pleased to remain behind, for the wild boar had often received them in a manner which did not make them desire its further acquaintance.

As soon as the boar perceived the tailor it ran at him with foaming mouth and gleaming teeth and tried to knock him down; but our alert little friend ran into a chapel that stood near and got out of the window again with a jump.

The boar pursued him into the church, but the tailor skipped round to the door, and closed it securely. So the raging beast was caught, for it was far too heavy and unwieldly to spring out of the window. The little tailor summoned the huntsmen together, that they might see the prisoner with their own eyes.

Then the hero betook himself to the King, who was obliged now, whether he liked it or not, to keep his promise, and hand

The Boar Ran at Him.

over his daughter and half his kingdom. Had he known that no hero-warrior, but only a little tailor, stood before him, it would have gone even more to his heart.

So the wedding was celebrated with much splendor but little joy, and the tailor became a King.

After a time the Queen heard her husband saying one night in his sleep: "My lad, make that waistcoat and patch those trousers, or I'll box your ears." Thus she learned in what rank the young gentleman had been born, and the next day she poured forth her woes to her father, and begged him to help her to get rid of a husband who was nothing more nor less than a tailor.

The King comforted her, and said: "Leave your bedroom door open to-night. My servants shall stand outside, and when your husband is fast asleep they shall enter, bind him fast, and carry him on to a ship, which shall sail away out into the wide ocean."

The Queen was well satisfied with the idea, but the armor-bearer, who had overheard everything, being much attached to his young master, went straight to him and revealed the whole plot.

"I'll soon put a stop to the business," said the tailor. That night he and his wife went to bed at the usual time; when she thought he had fallen asleep she got up, opened the door, and then lay down again.

The little tailor, who had only pretended to be asleep, began to call out in a clear voice: "My lad, make that waistcoat and patch those trousers, or I'll box your ears. I have killed seven at one blow,

So the Tailor Became a King.

slain two giants, led a unicorn captive, and caught a wild boar. Why should I be afraid of those men standing outside my door?"

The men, when they heard the tailor saying these words, were so terrified that they fled as if pursued by a wild army, and didn't dare go near him again. So the little tailor was and remained a King all the days of his life!

They Fled As If Pursued by an Army.

Under Every Tree Lay a Lion.

THE · SEVEN-HEADED · SERPENT

O nce upon a time there was a King who determined to take a long voyage. He assembled his fleet and all the seamen, and set out. They went straight on night and day, until they came to an island which was covered with large trees, and under every tree lay a lion. As soon as the King had landed his men, the lions all rose up together and tried to devour them. After a long battle they managed to overcome the wild beasts, but the greater number of the men were killed.

Those who remained alive now went on through the forest and found on the other side of it a beautiful garden, in which all the plants of the world flourished together. There were also in the garden three springs: the first flowed with silver, the second with gold, and the third with pearls. The men unbuckled their knapsacks and filled them with those precious things. In the middle of the garden they found a large lake, and when they reached the edge of it the lake began to speak, and said to them, "What men are you, and what brings you here? Are you come to visit our King?"

But they were too much frightened to answer.

Then the lake said, "You do well to be afraid, for it is at your peril that you are come hither. Our King, who has seven heads, is now asleep, but in a few minutes he will wake up and come to me to take his bath! Woe to anyone who meets him in the garden, for it is impossible to escape from him. This is what you must do if you wish to save your lives. Take off your clothes and spread them on the path which leads from here to the castle. The King will then glide over something soft, which he likes very much, and he will be so pleased with that that he will not devour you. He will give you some punishment, but then he will let you go."

The men did as the lake advised them, and waited for a time. At noon the earth began to quake, and opened in many places, and out of the openings appeared lions, tigers, and other wild beasts, which surrounded the castle, and thousands and thousands of beasts came out of the castle following their King, the Seven-headed Serpent. The Serpent glided over the clothes which were spread for him, came to the lake, and asked it who had strewed those soft things on the path?

The lake answered that it had been done by people who had come to do him homage. The King commanded that the men should be brought before him. They came humbly on their knees, and in a few words told him their story.

Then he spoke to them with a mighty and terrible voice, and said, "Because you have dared to come here, I lay upon you pun-

The Men Did as the Lake Advised Them.

ishment. Every year you must bring me from among your people twelve youths and twelve maidens, that I may devour them. If you do not do this, I will destroy your whole nation."

Then he desired one of his beasts to show the men the way out of the garden, and dismissed them. They left the island and went back to their own country, where they related what had happened to them. Soon the time came round when the King of the Beasts would expect the youths and maidens to be brought to him. The King therefore issued a proclamation inviting twelve youths and twelve maidens to offer themselves up to save their country; and immediately many young people, far more than enough, hastened to do so. A new ship was built, and set with black sails, and in it the youths and maidens who were appointed for the King of the Beasts embarked and set out for his country.

When they arrived there they went at once to the lake, and this time the lions did not stir, nor did the springs flow, and neither did the lake speak. So they waited then, and it was not long before the earth quaked even more terribly than the first time. The Seven-headed Serpent came with his train of beasts, saw his prey waiting for him, and devoured it at one mouthful. Then the ship's crew returned home, and the same thing happened yearly until many years had passed.

Now the King of this unhappy country was growing old, and so was the Queen, and they had no children. One day the Queen was sitting at the window weeping bitterly because she was child-

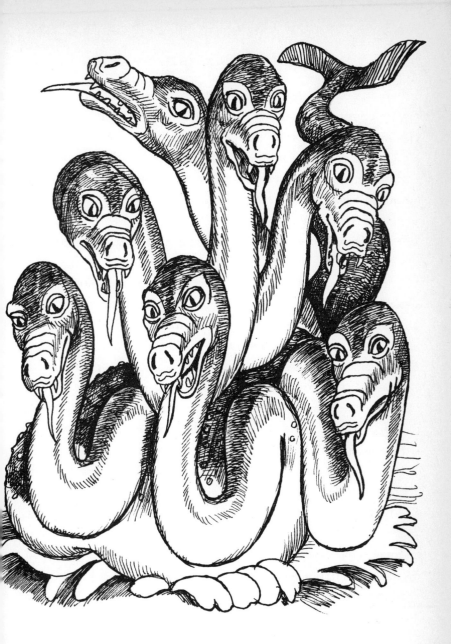

"I Will Destroy Your Whole Nation."

less, and knew that the crown would therefore pass to strangers after the King's death. Suddenly a little old woman appeared before her, holding an apple in her hand, and said, "Why do you weep, my Queen, and what makes you so unhappy?"

"Alas, good mother," answered the Queen, "I am unhappy because I have no children."

"Is that what vexes you?" said the old woman. "Listen to me. My mother when she died left me this apple. Whoever eats this apple shall have a child."

The Queen gave money to the old woman, and bought the apple from her. Then she peeled it, ate it, and threw the rind out of the window, and it so happened that a mare that was running loose in the court below ate up the rind.

After a time the Queen had a little boy, and the mare also had a male foal. The boy and the foal grew up together and loved each other like brothers. In the course of time the King died, and so did the Queen, and their son, who was now nineteen years old, was left alone.

One day, when he and his horse were talking together, the horse said to him, "Listen to me, for I love you and wish for your good and that of the country. If you go on every year sending twelve youths and twelve maidens to the King of the Beasts, your country will very soon be ruined. Mount upon my back: I will take you to a woman who can direct you how to kill the Seven-headed Serpent."

A Little Old Woman Appeared Before the Queen.

Then the youth mounted his horse, who carried him far away to a mountain which was hollow, for in its side was a great underground cavern. In the cavern sat an old woman spinning. The cavern was a cloister of the nuns, and the old woman was the Abbess. They all spent their time in spinning.

All round the walls of the cavern there were beds cut out of the solid rock, upon which the nuns slept, and in the middle a light was burning. It was the duty of the nuns to watch the light in turns, that it might never go out, and if anyone of them let it go out the others would put her to death.

As soon as the King's son saw the old Abbess spinning, he threw himself at her feet and entreated her to tell him how he could kill the Seven-headed Serpent.

She made the youth rise, embraced him, and said, "Know, my son, that it is I who sent a nun to your mother and caused you to be born, and with you the horse, with whose help you will be able to free the world from the monster.

"I will tell you what you have to do. Load your horse with cotton, and go by a secret passage which I will show you, which is hidden from the wild beasts, to the Serpent's palace. You will find the King asleep upon his bed, which is all hung round with bells, and over his bed you will see a sword hanging. With this sword only is it possible to kill the Serpent, because even if its blade breaks a new one will grow again for every head the monster has. Thus you will be able to cut off all his seven heads. And this you

His Horse Carried Him to a Hollow Mountain.

must also do in order to deceive the Serpent: you must slip into his bed chamber very softly, and stop up all the bells which are round his bed with cotton. Then take down the sword gently, and quickly give the monster a blow on his tail with it. This will make him wake up, and if he catches sight of you he will seize you. But you must quickly cut off his first head, and then wait till the next one comes up. Then strike it off also, and so go on till you have cut off all his seven heads."

The old Abbess then gave the Prince her blessing, and he set out upon his enterprise, arrived at the Serpent's castle by following the secret passage which she had shown him, and by carefully attending to all her directions he happily succeeded in killing the monster. As soon as the wild beasts heard of their King's death, they all hastened to the castle, but the youth had long since mounted his horse and was already far out of their reach. They pursued him as fast as they could, but they found it impossible to overtake him, and he reached home in safety. Thus he freed his country from terrible oppression.

"Take Down the Sword Gently."

"I Will Bring You Good Luck!"

THE · TWO · BROTHERS

Long ago there lived two brothers, both of them very handsome, and both so very poor that they seldom had anything to eat but the fish which they caught. One day they had been out in their boat since sunrise without a single bite, and were just thinking of putting up their lines and going home to bed when they felt a little feeble tug, and, drawing in hastily, they found a tiny fish at the end of the hook.

"What a wretched little creature!" cried one brother. "However, it is better than nothing, and I will bake him with bread crumbs and have him for supper."

"Oh, do not kill me yet!" begged the fish; "I will bring you good luck — indeed I will!"

"You silly thing!" said the young man; "I've caught you, and I shall eat you."

But his brother was sorry for the fish, and put in a word for him.

"Let the poor little fellow live. He would hardly make one

bite, and, after all, how do we know we are not throwing away our luck? Put him back into the sea. It will be much better."

"If you will let me live," said the fish, "you will find on the sands to-morrow morning two beautiful horses splendidly saddled and bridled, and on them you can go through the world as knights seeking adventures."

"Oh dear, what nonsense!" exclaimed the elder; "and, besides, what proof have we that you are speaking the truth?"

But again the younger brother interposed: "Oh, do let him live! You know if he is lying to us we can always catch him again. It is quite worthwhile trying."

At last the elder brother gave in, and threw the fish back into the sea; and both brothers went supperless to bed, and wondered what fortune the next day would bring.

At the first streaks of dawn they were both up, and in a very few minutes were running down to the shore. And there, just as the fish had said, stood two magnificent horses, saddled and bridled, and on their backs lay suits of armor and under-garments, two swords, and two purses of gold.

"There!" said the younger brother. "Are you not thankful you did not eat that fish? He has brought us good luck, and there is no knowing how great we may become! Now, we will each seek our own adventures. If you will take one road I will go the other."

"Very well," replied the elder; "but how shall we let each other know if we are both living?"

Running Down to the Shore

"Do you see this fig tree?" said the younger. "Well, whenever we want news of each other we have only to come here and make a slit with our swords in the bark. If milk flows, it is a sign that we are well and prosperous; but if, instead of milk, there is blood, then we are either dead or in great danger."

Then the two brothers put on their armor, buckled their swords, and pocketed their purses; and, after taking a tender farewell of each other, they mounted their horses and went their separate ways.

The elder brother rode straight on till he reached the borders of a strange kingdom. He crossed the frontier, and soon found himself on the banks of a river; and before him, in the middle of the stream, a beautiful girl sat chained to a rock, weeping bitterly. For in this river dwelt a monster with three tails, great thwacking things, who threatened to lay waste the whole land with them unless the King sent him a man for his breakfast every morning. This had gone on so long that now there were no men left, and he had been obliged to send his own daughter instead, and the poor girl was waiting till the monster got hungry and felt inclined to eat her.

When the young man saw the maiden weeping bitterly he said to her, "What is the matter, my poor girl?"

"Oh!" she answered, "I am chained here till a horrible monster with three great tails comes to eat me. Oh, sir, do not linger here, or he will eat you, too."

"If Milk Flows . . ."

"I shall stay," replied the young man, "for I mean to set you free."

"That is impossible. You do not know what a fearful monster he is; you can do nothing against him."

"That is my affair, beautiful captive," answered he; "only tell me, which way will the monster come?"

"Well, if you are resolved to free me, listen to my advice. Stand a little on one side, and then, when the monster rises to the surface, I will say to him, 'O monster, today you can eat two people. But you had better begin first with the young man, for I am chained and cannot run away.' When he hears this, most likely he will attack you."

So the young man stood carefully on one side, and by and by he heard a great rushing in the water; and a horrible monster came up to the surface and looked out for the rock where the King's daughter was chained, for it was getting late and he was hungry.

But she cried out, "O monster, today you can eat two people. And you had better begin with the young man, for I am chained and cannot run away."

Then the monster made a rush at the youth with wide open jaws to swallow him at one gulp, but the young man leaped aside and drew his sword, and fought till he had cut off all the monster's tails and his head. And when the great monster lay dead at his feet he loosed the bonds of the King's daughter, and she flung herself into his arms and said, "You have saved me from that monster, and

The Horrible Monster Came Up to the Surface.

now you shall be my husband, for my father has made a proclamation that whoever could slay the monster should have his daughter to wife."

But he answered, "I cannot become your husband yet, for I have still far to travel. But wait for me seven years and seven months. Then, if I do not return, you are free to marry whom you will. And in case you should have forgotten, I will take these tail ends with me, so that when I bring them forth you may know that I am really he who slew the monster."

So saying he cut off the tails, and the Princess gave him a thick cloth to wrap them in; and he mounted his horse and rode away.

Not long after he had gone, there arrived at the river a slave who had been sent by the King to learn the fate of his beloved daughter. And when the slave saw the Princess standing free and safe before him, with the body of the monster lying at her feet, a wicked plan came into his head, and he said, "Unless you promise to tell your father it was I who slew the monster, I will kill you and bury you in this place, and no one will ever know what befell."

What could the poor girl do? This time there was no knight to come to her aid. So she promised to do as the slave wished, and he took up the three tails and brought the Princess to her father.

Oh, how enchanted the King was to see her again, and the whole town shared his joy!

And the slave was called upon to tell how he had slain the monster, and when he had ended the King declared that he should

"Wait for Me Seven Years and Seven Months."

have the Princess to wife.

But she flung herself at her father's feet, and prayed him to delay. "You have given your royal word, and cannot go back from it. Yet grant me this grace, and let seven years and seven months go by before you wed me. When they are over, I will marry the slave."

And the King listened to her, and seven years and seven months she looked for her bridegroom, and wept for him night and day.

All this time the young man was riding through the world, and when the seven years and seven months were over he came back to the town where the Princess lived — only a few days before the wedding. And he stood before the King, and said to him: "Give me your daughter, O King, for I slew the three tailed monster. And as a sign that my words are true, look on these tails, which I cut from him, and on this embroidered cloth, which was given me by your daughter."

Then the Princess lifted up her voice and said, "Yes, dear father, he has spoken the truth, and it is he who is my real bridegroom. Yet pardon the slave, for he was sorely tempted."

But the King answered, "Such treachery can no man pardon. Quick, away with him, and off with his head!"

So the false slave was put to death, that none might follow in his footsteps, and the wedding feast was held, and the hearts of all rejoiced that the true bridegroom had come at last.

These two lived happy and contentedly for a long while,

"Yet Grant Me This Grace."

when one evening, as the young man was looking from the window, he saw on a mountain that lay out beyond the town a great bright light.

"What can it be?" he said to his wife.

"Ah! Do not look at it," she answered, "for it comes from the house of a wicked witch whom no man can manage to kill." But the Princess had better have kept silent, for her words made her husband's heart burn within him, and he longed to try his strength against the witch's cunning. And all day long the feeling grew stronger, till the next morning he mounted his horse, and, in spite of his wife's tears, he rode off to the mountain. The distance was greater than he thought, and it was dark before he reached the foot of the mountain; indeed, he could not have found the road at all had it not been for the bright light, which shone like the moon on his path. At length he came to the door of a fine castle, which had a blaze streaming from every window. He mounted a flight of steps and entered a hall where a hideous old woman was sitting on a golden chair.

She scowled at the young man and said, "With a single one of the hairs of my head I can turn you into stone."

"Oh, what nonsense!" cried he. "Be quiet, old woman. What could you do with one hair?" But the witch pulled out a hair and laid it on his shoulder, and his limbs grew cold and heavy, and he could not stir.

Now at this very moment the younger brother was thinking

He Saw a Great Bright Light.

of him, and wondering how he had got on during all the years since they had parted. "I will go to the fig tree," he said to himself, "to see whether he is alive or dead."

So he rode through the forest till he came to where the fig tree stood, and cut a slit in the bark, and waited. In a moment a little gurgling noise was heard, and out came a stream of blood, running fast. "Ah, woe is me!" he cried bitterly. "My brother is dead or dying! Shall I ever reach him in time to save his life?" Then, leaping on his horse, he shouted, "Now, my steed, fly like the wind!" and they rode right through the world, till one day they came to the town where the young man and his wife lived.

Here the Princess had been sitting every day since the morning that her husband had left her, weeping bitter tears, and listening for his footsteps.

And when she saw his brother ride under the balcony she mistook him for her own husband, for they were so alike that no man might tell the difference, and her heart bounded, and, leaning down, she called to him, "At last! At last! How long have I waited for thee!"

When the younger brother heard these words he said to himself, "So it was here that my brother lived, and this beautiful woman is my sister-in-law," but he kept silent, and let her believe he was indeed her husband.

Full of joy, the Princess led him to the old King, who welcomed him as his own son, and ordered a feast to be made for him.

"I Will Go to the Fig Tree."

And the Princess was beside herself with gladness, but when she would have put her arms round him and kissed him he held up his hand to stop her, saying, "Touch me not," at which she marvelled greatly.

In this manner several days went by. And one evening, as the young man leaned from the balcony, he saw a bright light shining on the mountain.

"What can that be?" he said to the Princess.

"Oh, come away," she cried; "has not that light already proved your bane? Do you wish to fight a second time with that old witch?"

He marked her words, though she knew it not, and they taught him where his brother was, and what had befallen him. So before sunrise he stole out early, saddled his horse, and rode off to the mountain. But the way was further than he thought, and on the road he met a little old man who asked him whither he was going.

Then the young man told him his story, and added, "Somehow or other I must free my brother, who has fallen into the power of an old witch."

"I will tell you what you must do," said the old man. "The witch's power lies in her hair; so when you see her, spring on her and seize her by the hair, and then she cannot harm you. Be very careful never to let her hair go, bid her lead you to your brother, and force her to bring him back to life. For she has an ointment that will heal all wounds, and even wake the dead. And when your

"Touch Me Not."

brother stands safe and well before you, then cut off her head, for she is a wicked woman."

The young man was grateful for these words, and promised to obey them. Then he rode on, and soon reached the castle. He walked boldly up the steps and entered the hall, where the hideous old witch came to meet him. She grinned horribly at him, and cried out, "With one hair of my head I can change you into stone."

"Can you, indeed?" said the young man, seizing her by the hair. "You old wretch! Tell me what you have done with my brother, or I will cut your head off this very instant." Now the witch's strength was all gone from her, and she had to obey.

"I will take you to your brother," she said, hoping to get the better of him by cunning, "but leave me alone. You hold me so tight that I cannot walk."

"You must manage somehow," he answered, and held her tighter than ever. She led him into a large hall filled with stone statues, which once had been men, and, pointing out one, she said, "There is your brother."

The young man looked at them all and shook his head. "My brother is not here. Take me to him, or it will be the worse for you." But she tried to put him off with other statues, and it was not until they had reached the last hall of all that he saw his brother lying on the ground.

"*That* is my brother," said he. "Now give me the ointment that will restore him to life."

The Old Witch Came Out to Meet Him.

Very unwillingly the old witch opened a cupboard filled with bottles and jars, and took down one and held it out to the young man. But he was on the watch for trickery, and examined it carefully, and saw that it had no power to heal. This happened many times, till at length she found it was no use, and gave him the one he wanted.

And when he had it safe he made her stoop down and smear it over his brother's face, taking care all the while never to loose her hair, and when the dead man opened his eyes the youth drew his sword and cut off her head with a single blow.

Then the elder brother got up and stretched himself, and said, "Oh, how long I have slept! And where am I?"

"The old witch had enchanted you, but now she is dead and you are free. We will wake up the other knights that she laid under her spells, and then we will go."

This they did, and, after sharing amongst them the jewels and gold they found in the castle, each man went his way. The two brothers remained together, the elder tightly grasping the ointment which had brought him back to life.

They had much to tell each other as they rode along, and at last the younger man exclaimed, "O fool, to leave such a beautiful wife to go and fight a witch! She took me for her husband, and I did not say her nay."

When the elder brother heard this a great rage filled his heart, and, without saying one word, he drew his sword and slew his

Very Unwillingly, She Opened the Cupboard.

brother, and his body rolled in the dust. Then he rode on till he reached his home, where his wife was still sitting, weeping bitterly.

When she saw him she sprang up with a cry, and threw herself into his arms. "Oh, how long I have waited for thee! Never, never must you leave me any more!"

When the old King heard the news he welcomed him as a son, and made ready a feast, and all the court sat down. And in the evening, when the young man was alone with his wife, she said to him, "Why would you not let me touch you when you came back, but always thrust me away when I tried to put my arms around you or kiss you?"

Then the young man understood how true his brother had been to him, and he sat down and wept and wrung his hands because of the wicked murder that he had done. Suddenly he sprang to his feet, for he remembered the ointment which lay hidden in his garments, and he rushed to the place where his brother still lay.

He fell on his knees beside the body, and, taking out the salve, he rubbed it over the neck where the wound was gaping wide, and the skin healed and the sinews grew strong, and the dead man sat up and looked around him.

And the two brothers embraced each other, and the elder asked forgiveness for his wicked blow; and they went back to the palace together, and were never parted any more.

"How Long I Have Waited for Thee!"